A MESSAGE FROM CHICKEN HOUSE

I dream *a lot* – and sometimes it feels real. *The Ice Garden* is a novel trapped in that magical place between dreaming and waking. Jess finds the garden through a sense of longing – and lack of belonging – and soon she wishes she never had to leave. But what about the mysterious boy she encounters in this other world, and the strange darkness haunting the ice? Guy Jones tells a moving, dizzying tale – sometimes funny, sometimes sad. Brilliant and beautiful.

BARRY CUNNINGHAM
Publisher
Chicken House

2 Palmer Street, Frome, Somerset BA11 1DS
www.chickenhousebooks.com

First published in Great Britain in 2018
Chicken House
2 Palmer Street
Frome, Somerset BA11 1DS
United Kingdom
www.chickenhousebooks.com

Cover and interior design by Helen Crawford-White
Typeset by Dorchester Typesetting Group Ltd
Printed and bound in Great Britain by CPI Group (UK) Ltd, Croydon CR0 4YY

The paper used in this Chicken House book is made
from wood grown in sustainable forests.

1 3 5 7 9 10 8 6 4 2

British Library Cataloguing in Publication data available.

PB ISBN 978-1-911490-04-3
eISBN 978-1-911490-06-7

For Isabelle

They called it the Hat. It was a long white hood that masked the whole of Jess's face and neck, over which she wore something like ski goggles. The rest of her body was covered up with a baggy top, trousers and thick gloves so that no part of her skin was exposed to the sun.

'I don't like it here,' she said, lifting the goggles to get at a maddening itch on her nose.

'No one likes hospitals,' replied her mother.

'So, we can go?'

'You're in one of those moods, then.'

Jess sighed, releasing a mouthful of sickly air. The numbers on the lift display began ticking up towards the children's ward. Already, beads of sweat were forming on the back of her neck, sticking fabric to skin. Summer was the absolute worst time of year.

'It's only a couple of times a month,' said her mother.

'*Only?*' said Jess, her voice rising.

'Must we do this?'

Jess thought they probably must. At least until her mother understood how much she hated this building and everything in it.

The doors opened on the second floor to reveal a woman in a purple dress. She took a step towards them but stopped short at the sight of the Hat. Her mouth gaped like a fish but no words came out.

'Can we help?' asked Jess's mother.

'Oh . . .' she said, recovering herself a little. 'Up or down?'

'Going up.'

'Right. Well. Down for me. Thanks.' The woman took a step back, still staring.

'You can close your mouth now,' Jess said, as the lift doors closed.

'Darling, that was rude,' her mother scolded.

'She didn't hear me.'

'Shame.' They both smiled, without looking at one another. Her mother jabbed the fourth-floor button a few times and tapped her foot. The lift clunked and juddered as it started up again.

'I don't like him,' said Jess.

'He's perfectly nice.'

'He's nice to you. He talks to me like I'm an idiot.'

'He talks to you like you're a child.'

'Exactly.'

'He's a very good doctor.'

'How do you know? You don't have medical training.'

Game, set and match, Jess thought.

'Put your goggles back on,' said her mother. 'There are windows in the corridor.'

'But, Mum . . .' she started.

'Jessica,' her mother replied, firmly. *Game, set and match.*

Doctor Stannard was extremely tall, extremely thin and, Jess thought, extremely annoying. He had a habit of leaning forward at the waist, like a flagpole bending in the wind. He was so large that surely his father had been a giant – not just an ordinary person who happened to be on the big side, but a genuine giant like the ones you read about in books. Jess had written a story like that herself once, about a particularly nasty character who lived in a cave stacked high with the bones of unfortunate passers-by.

Doctor Stannard didn't look like he'd ever lived in a cave. Perhaps his giant parents had decided to modernize? If so, then every day would have been a struggle not to eat the postman, she thought.

Her own father, as far as she could remember, was relatively normal-sized. In the absence of clear answers from her mother, Jess had formed her own conclusions as to where he had gone. If asked, she'd explain that he was the unfortunate victim of alien abduction and that a shadowy government agency – for government agencies are always shadowy – had tried to keep this fact locked tightly away.

'Jess?' It was Doctor Stannard.

'Yes?'

'Doctor asked you to take your gloves off,' said her mother.

'Right,' she said.

'She was miles away, Mummy,' said the doctor. He always called her mother 'Mummy'. It was idiotic. 'You were miles away, weren't you, Jess?'

'I suppose so,' she said.

'What were you thinking about?' he asked.

'Puppies,' she replied.

Her mother shot her a look that said *I don't know what you were thinking about, darling, but I'd bet our house that it wasn't puppies*, but Doctor Stannard seemed happy enough.

He took her hand and turned it this way and that, rolling up the sleeve to look at her arm. When he was done, he moved to the other side. 'And what's this?' he said.

'What's what?' replied Jess, with an innocent smile.

'What is it?' asked her mother, concerned.

'Well, that's not good to see, is it, Jess? No, very nasty.'

Her mother leant over with the doctor and Jess looked down at the tops of the two adult heads as they peered at a patch of burnt skin on her wrist. 'I barely even felt it,' she protested.

It had happened a few days before. Her mother had been in the kitchen at the back of the house when shouting had started in the street outside. Mr Olmos from number thirty-three was on the pavement screaming at the postman, who, he said, had yet again failed to deliver his new ice-cream-making machine. The postman tried to make the point that he could not, in fact, deliver an item that hadn't yet arrived at the sorting office, but Mr Olmos hadn't wanted to listen. The postman was certainly an incompetent fool and, very possibly, the kind of scoundrel who'd steal another man's ice-cream maker.

Jess had pulled on the Hat and opened the door to listen. The downstairs windows were tinted but whenever she ventured outside she had to make sure she went 'Full Hat', as her mother put it. She liked Mr Olmos. He was a restless man, who caught new hobbies like other people catch colds. This month it was making his own ice cream, the one before it had been learning the harmonica, and a few weeks before that he had attempted to build a small working rocket in his front garden. Jess suspected that even he'd been a little bit relieved when that one hadn't worked.

Watching the scene unfold, she'd reached down to scratch an itch on her arm. Her bare arm. She'd jumped back into the hall, slamming the door. Looking down, she could see where her sleeve had snagged, revealing a smooth white patch of skin. After just a few short minutes in the sun the spot had flared up into a nest of angry red blisters.

'What was that?' her mother had said, coming into the hall.

'Mr Olmos is angry about ice cream,' Jess had replied.

Her mother shook her head. 'That man.'

'I like him.'

'You can peel the potatoes,' she'd said, heading back to the kitchen.

Jess had pulled her sleeve down and gone through without complaint.

'Jess . . .' said her mother, fingers worrying at a loose strand of hair. 'If I can't trust you to look after yourself . . . I can't watch you every moment!'

'You don't need to.'

'You went outside in the day!'

'I was covered up.'

'Not well enough.'

'My sleeve got stuck – it's not like I did it on purpose.'

'Don't take that tone.'

'I'm not taking any tone.'

Her mother glanced up at Doctor Stannard, who was looking at them with an expression that screamed, *I understand*, and made Jess want to hit him with his own stapler.

'What do you think, Doctor?' sighed her mother.

'I think she needs to be careful, Mummy. Very careful indeed.'

'You hear what Doctor says, Jess?'

She opened her mouth to respond, to shout at them both that it had been an accident, that she *was* careful, that she was *always* careful. Instead she set her face and stood. 'Can I go?' she asked.

'Go where?'

'For a walk. You can talk about me more easily if I'm not here.' Her mother's glance was knifelike. 'Please,' Jess added.

'You'll have to go Full Hat.'

'I know that.' Jess snatched the hood up from a plastic-looking desk.

Her mother slipped back into the chair with a sigh. 'Five minutes, then,' she said, 'no more.'

Jess gave a sharp military salute and let the door swing shut behind her.

3

She pulled on her goggles and scowled as the orange lenses made the world just that little bit duller. A sad painted rainbow arced across one wall of the corridor. An orderly came by pushing a wheelchair that chirped like a small bird. In it was an elderly woman who looked her up and down. 'You poor thing,' she said as she passed. 'Everything will be OK.'

Jess knew that adults found it difficult to see her in Full Hat. Most likely they had no idea why a child had to dress up in an outfit best suited to tending bees. In any case, it was obvious to them that that *this child isn't normal* and is therefore *in need of my sympathy*. Jess didn't want anyone's sympathy. She had what she needed. Her mother, for one thing. Her maddening, frustrating, wonderful mother.

And of course she had her stories. Just that morning she had added another entry to her *Big Book of Tales*. This creation would one day make her rich and famous, at which point she would buy a better desk so that she could embark on her dream of writing an *Even Bigger Book of Tales*.

She navigated a few turns but each hallway looked much the same as the last. Fluorescent lights cast a blue-green tinge. Here and there rows of orange plastic chairs were bolted to the walls. She came to a window. A shaft of sunlight cut through the glass and Jess let it play across her gloves, feeling a familiar shudder of desire and fear. *I could take them off*, she thought, and imagined how furious Doctor Stannard would be if she did. She was snapped from her fantasy when a football thudded into the glass pane in front of her.

She peered down to see a group of children in the road below. One of them, a scrawny boy, was climbing into the flower beds by the hospital wall to rummage under the bushes there. His friends milled around, conducting their conversation as loudly as if they were at opposite ends of the street rather than standing right next to each other.

'Get a move on!' one of the girls shouted. She had the same sandy-blonde hair as the boy. *His sister*, Jess thought. There was a yelp from under the bushes and he emerged with livid red welts on his arms, looking every bit as deflated as the football he was holding.

'What did I say about kicking it?' the girl barked. 'You're going home to get another.' The boy started to protest but was quickly shouted down. Only when he jogged away did the rest of the group move off towards the park at the end of the road.

There was a familiar hollow feeling in Jess's chest, as if someone had been to work inside it with an ice-cream scoop. The sandy-haired girl stopped, falling behind the others, and went down on one knee to retie her shoes. She looked interesting, Jess thought. Her clothes were too big and her jeans were worn through and grass-stained at the knees. What would the girl make of Jess introducing herself, she wondered? What would it be like to spend the afternoon with them, kicking the ball around in the sunshine, teasing each other, talking about whatever came into their heads? She found herself smiling – a smile that bubbled up like foam from a bottle of fizzy drink and vanished just as quickly. Because at that moment the girl looked up and saw her.

Jess lifted a hand in greeting but the girl on the street below didn't move or return the gesture. At that moment a broken fragment of cloud passed in front of the sun and Jess could see her own reflection in the window – could see herself as the girl saw her. Could see that her face was masked and that her waving hand was clad in a thick white glove.

She jerked back from the window, wanting nothing more than to be invisible. Her face and chest burnt red-hot, and she could hear the blood pumping in her ears. No wonder she hadn't waved back. Jess didn't even look like a little girl. She was different. She was *strange*.

4

A nurse with a greying shock of wire-wool hair hurried out of the room opposite and away down the corridor. As the door swung shut Jess caught a glimpse of a boy lying inside. On impulse, and checking that the hall was empty, she ducked through.

The room was empty apart from the figure in the bed. He looked about her age. There was a vase of yellow flowers on the side and the windowsill was crowded with get-well-soon cards. She fixed one, which had fallen over. It showed a floppy-eared baby mouse wrapped up in quilts and blankets, with a thermometer in its mouth. The boy himself was lying perfectly still. Tubes snaked into him from a variety of machines. Green lights flashed and a steady beep tapped out a deadening rhythm. Jess drew the blinds and pulled off her hood and goggles: Half Hat. At once her nostrils filled with the reek of pollen. She dipped her head and breathed deeply, allowing the scent to overwhelm the sharp antiseptic tang of the hospital.

A photograph was propped up on the bedside table. In it a family stood on a rickety-looking jetty that extended across a frozen lake. Frost-covered flower beds lay in the foreground while snowy mountains reared up in the distance. Sunlight played across the ice and Jess felt a sudden pressure and tightness in her chest. She pushed the sadness away and turned to the boy.

He was almost as colourless as Jess herself. Spider-webs of blue veins showed through the too-pale skin at his temples. His chest rose and fell with a faint hissing sound. He was thin – thinner than in the photo. There he was grinning into the camera while on either side of him his parents were laughing at something out of shot.

Who was he? *The son of a spy*, she thought. His father – no, his mother – worked for the government in some of the most dangerous places in the world. She spoke eight languages, was a black belt in judo and could do twelve backflips in a row. It seemed obvious to Jess that such a woman had almost certainly trained her son to follow in her footsteps. At the age of just twelve, he could already shoot the top off a bottle from a hundred metres, fly a helicopter, and survive in the wild with only a cagoule and a tin of beans.

What had brought him here? Well, that was obvious. His mother had been investigating corruption at the highest levels when she'd been discovered. Agents had been sent to capture her family and even though she'd fought them off with nothing but the contents of a cutlery drawer, she hadn't been able to stop the bullet that had put her son in a coma . . .

All at once Jess felt very tired and buried her head in her hands. 'I'm sorry,' she said at last, her voice sounding thin and artificial in the hushed room. 'It must be awful, just lying there like that with all those things stuck into your arms. Hearing nothing but doctors and nurses talking about you all the time.'

For one mad moment she half expected the boy to answer, but of course there was nothing but the slow rasp of his breath. *Where are you?* she wondered. Had his mind floated off to some other place? Was he dreaming? Or was he just waiting? Waiting for something to change so that he could finally wake up.

She moved on to the side of the bed, feeling the mattress sag under her weight. 'I know how you feel a little bit. With the doctors, I mean. I come here every few weeks and all they do is talk about me, about how I am or what they want to do to me next. And no one ever asks me, not really. Do you know what I wish? I wish there was no sun, ever. No sun for anyone, and everyone the same as I am. Does that sound bad? To wish everyone else had to live in darkness too? Well, I don't care if it does.'

She pulled off one glove and reached down to take the boy's hand, half expecting to feel his fingers curl around her own. But there was nothing; they just rested there, still and cold. *So cold*, she thought. A sudden flutter of terror came upon her. How could a person have so little warmth in their body and yet still live? But then some would ask how a person could live without sun, as she did.

'I wouldn't,' she said at last. 'Make everyone else be like me. But I wish there was a place I could go. Somewhere safe.' She let out a long, sad breath.

There was a bag on the chair in the corner. Brown leather, beaten up. A woman's bag, much like the one her mother had. She could see a set of keys nestling inside its open mouth, which meant that whoever it belonged to had probably only gone out for a moment. Which meant they were most likely on their way back. Which meant she had to get out of there or risk having to explain herself.

'I hope you wake up soon,' she whispered, leaning over him. She swept away a strand of mousy hair that had fallen over his eyes. 'And I hope you have good dreams until then.'

She zigzagged back to Doctor Stannard's office only to find her mother already standing outside. 'I said five minutes.'

Jess nodded. This one wasn't worth fighting.

'We need to get that burn seen to.'

'I told you, it's fine.'

'It's a mess and you know it.'

'I don't want to.'

'And yet you still have to.' Her mother softened. 'Come on, little one, it'll only take a moment. Let's go and see the nurse and then we can go home.'

More poking and prodding, Jess thought. *More and more and more and more.* She'd had enough of it. She'd had enough. Something had to change.

5

Jess lay awake, listening for the arthritic creak of the stairs as her mother turned in for the night. A few minutes later the glow from beneath her door was extinguished, but still she waited. Street light streamed through the trees outside her window and threw shadows across her wall.

Only when she was sure the house was truly sleeping did she slip out of bed and into jeans and a T-shirt. She crept downstairs and paused at the front door, scarcely able to believe what she was about to do. *I think she needs to be careful, Mummy. Very careful indeed . . .* She cringed at the memory of Doctor Stannard's voice. Then she turned the handle and stepped out into the street. Her stomach unclenched a little and suddenly she was nothing more than a normal girl, in normal clothes, able to do as she pleased. Her heart began to race and she couldn't stop a grin from spreading across her face. *I'm doing it*, she thought, *I'm really doing it!*

The night air was soupy and warm, but she shivered as a slight breeze wrapped itself around her bare arms. In the winter months her mother often took her walking after dark, but in summer, when the sun didn't fall until after her bedtime, there was no such luck. Jess had argued that the normal rules shouldn't apply, but her mother had consulted Doctor Stannard, who had gone on for a while about the virtues of a good night's sleep.

She glanced back at her house, the same as every other on the street. A couple of steps led up to a black front door, above which two first-floor windows peered down at her like a pair of eyes. Her mother's room was on the left. *What if she wakes up?* Jess thought with a shudder. She could go back inside, it would be easy, but there was a whole town out there that she only ever saw from behind tinted car windows or the orange lenses of the Hat. And even worse was the way the town saw *her* – as something strange to be stared at and whispered about.

She blew out a slow breath and started down her road: a thin strip of tarmac sandwiched between red-brick terraces, at the end of which was a corner shop. The place had a bright blue sign that should have been cheery but somehow looked plain miserable.

That's far enough, she told herself. It was the middle of the night, so that *had to be* far enough. And yet she kept on going, through the maze of houses and on to the High Street itself. There was a drumbeat playing in her head, getting faster and louder with a growing excitement she could barely keep concealed.

The shops were all sleeping, their shutters like closed eyelids casting a tarnished reflection of the street lamps. She knew that in the day it would be full of people, but the town was a different place at night. Gaudy rubbish clogged the gutters and the air was thick with the scent of fried food and vinegar.

She wasn't surprised that people stared – a young girl out at night is unusual, after all, and she was small for her age to boot. A middle-aged man and woman, hand in hand, stopped and for a moment she was terrified they'd ask where her parents were. She didn't break stride, walking as if she had every right to be there, but thought herself very small. As she passed them she felt the couple's eyes slide off her. She smiled to herself. She was all right. She was all but invisible.

Weston Road traced its way downhill, from the High Street to the better part of town. It was lined on one side by large houses and on the other by railings. Beyond those was a slope spattered with low trees and bushes. At the bottom lay a park where street lamps threw strange shapes across the grey grass. A small lake glinted like a silver-black mirror.

Jess rested her hands on the bars, refreshingly cool in the muggy air. From her vantage point she could see a half-lit playground tucked away in one corner near the playing fields. At this time of night, it was a dead thing. The metal equipment was as bare as sun-bleached animal bones, stranded and forgotten in the desert.

The gate groaned as she pushed it and made her way down the zigzag path. She settled on one of the swings and began to rock herself back and forth, her shoes sending up puffs of dust as they scuffed the ground. *It's better than nothing*, she thought, as if sitting there in the lamplight would give her some small part of what she missed out on in the day.

She could imagine them if she tried – those daytime children. They jumped into her mind's eye as easily as the characters in her stories and she spoke out loud, narrating the scene as if reading from a book. There, on the seesaw, a brother and sister – twins by the look of them. The woman next to them almost certainly their mother, all three sharing the same thick black hair. Two small boys forced the mother to dodge aside as they pelted by making police-siren noises. The woman's lips pursed and she shook her head slightly.

On the other side, an Indian girl with a megawatt smile was being urged higher and higher on the climbing frame by a younger blonde friend; a father tried in vain to coax a screaming toddler on to the slide; three mothers sat in a line on the bench, each with one eye on their phone and the other on their child. The shouts, cries and laughter merged together into a beautiful and bizarre racket. The playground was alive in a wonderful, disorderly whirl.

And then it wasn't. It was simply dark and empty. The chain ropes of the swings clicked and creaked in the breeze. She fell silent.

When Jess was small, her mother had arranged for other children to visit and play, but it had always been difficult. It was hard to stay friends with the little girl who couldn't go outside, who didn't go to school. She still remembered the day all that had come to a crushing end, when her two so-called friends had told her that they'd made up a song just for her. She'd grinned at them, happy that they'd thought to do that, and waited for them to begin.

Freaky Jess, she can't go out,
Can't go out and run about.
Freaky Jess must stay inside,
Freaky Jess, she has to hide.

Over and over they'd sung it until her eyes burnt with acid tears, but that just seemed to spur them on. At last, thankfully, her sobbing attracted her mother's attention. After that day two things changed: no more children had come round to play, and Jess had never again cried in front of strangers.

They're the type of kids who come here, she thought. They must have played amongst these metal frames. But never in the dead of night the way Jess had to. The playground they saw was not the same as hers.

There was a noise. She came to a stop, listening hard. Nothing. There was nothing, and yet a new drumbeat started up in the back of her head that sounded like *There's something wrong, there's something wrong.* Jess eased herself off the swing and peered at the narrow, tree-lined path that led to the main road above.

That was her route home. Was there something up there, waiting to jump out at her? *There's something wrong, there's something wrong,* went the drumbeat. Her neck prickled and she shivered as if struck by a blast of freezing air.

It could be anything. A fox or a rabbit. Or a . . . a something. *A something hiding and watching.* That was enough for her – panic hit like breakers swamping a boat and she cast around for another way out. The playground was ringed by conifer trees, all crammed in side by side. If she could slip through, she'd be able to run across the playing fields and back up to the road that way. She searched and found a slight gap that she could force her way into.

The sickly scent of the firs flooded her nose and mouth, as if the trees were shouting in their own language that there was an intruder in their midst. Dull green limbs scratched and prickled her skin. Even the needles carpeting the ground joined the struggle, shouting their protest with every crunch of her feet. She shielded her face and scooped branches out of the way, almost swimming through to the other side.

But there was no escape. She found herself in a narrow corridor with the trees at her back and an impenetrable laurel hedge in front. She imagined whatever was out there starting to cross the playground with heavy, wet steps – some dripping creature of the night. There was another sudden gust of icy wind, out of place on a summer's night.

She had to find a way through. She pushed along the corridor until finally, gratefully, she found a gap in the hedge. All she needed to do was get through to the playing fields on the other side and then run – run back to the road, through the town and into her bed.

She stepped through and into the impossible.

Jess's mind looped around, trying and failing to make sense of what was in front of her. It stuttered to a halt, unable to cope with something so strange and illogical. Then, slowly, it came back to life and, with it, a dawning sense of wonder. For, on stepping through the gap, the whole world around her had changed.

Firstly, the moon had vanished. It had been there just seconds before, but now it was nowhere to be seen. In fact, the whole sky was different. The familiar dark tablecloth, scattered with stars, had been replaced by a mottled twilit heaven, like the most glorious sunset imaginable. From a light mauve in the distance it thickened into a deep purple above her head. It was streaked with clouds that burnt at their edges despite the absence of a sun in the sky.

Secondly, her arms were puckered with goose bumps. The night air was no longer a smooth summer balm, but rather a sharp-edged, biting chill.

And finally, most remarkably of all, everything in front of her was glistening white. She took a few steps forwards and heard a delicate crunch beneath her trainers. Looking down, she saw she was walking on a lawn, but instead of grass there were blades of frost. Looking back, she could see the footsteps of crushed ice she'd left in her wake.

She was in a garden, she realized. But one completely made of ice. Which is not to say that it was *covered* in ice, like a normal garden on a frosty morning or after a snowfall. Rather, every tree, leaf, rock, flower and blade of grass was composed completely and entirely *of* ice.

Jess closed her eyes, ready for the mirage to have vanished when she opened them again. But it was still there. It was real. Her breath turned to steam in the bitter air. She felt as if there was a taut string running through her, vibrating at a pitch somewhere between terror and joy.

Behind her a huge white wall rose up beyond the limits of her vision. In the middle was the thin crack through which she'd come. The ice was solid and strangely smooth to the touch, and looked as if it might go on for miles. Yet, when she stepped back through the gap, it proved to be no more than a few centimetres thick. The other side was the same as it had been: a laurel hedge with fir trees close behind. It was summer and a fat moon still hung in the sky. In fact, everything around her was just . . . normal. Yet when she went back through the gap in the hedge, the world was utterly changed. It was like looking at a car, then walking around to the other side to discover it was actually an elephant. Both states seemed to be completely real – no fakery or tricks of the light.

This can't be right, Jess thought. *This is just . . .* But what was it? What could possibly explain the evidence of her own eyes?

She examined the gap itself, and saw that the ice had formed around the branches of the hedge, which jutted out in places. At ground level there was even a crushed drinks can held beneath the surface like an ancient insect trapped in amber. There was no other explanation for it – this gap was where two worlds merged. On one side was everything she was familiar with and on the other some kind of ice garden.

It was perfectly quiet, so much so it was almost unnerving. In the town you could always hear the rumble of far-off traffic or the whine of aircraft in the sky above. But the silence of the ice garden was as pristine as the air itself. No sounds from her own world leaked through. She was utterly alone, she realized.

There was no one to disturb her. *And no one to tell me what to do.*

She hugged herself and rubbed her arms, trying to get some warmth back into them. For a moment she thought of running home for a coat and jumper, but what if she couldn't find the spot again? Or worse, what if the entrance somehow closed itself up while she was gone? She thrust her hands deep into her pockets and forged ahead along the main path, ignoring the smaller tracks that occasionally sprouted from either side. The ice around her, she saw, was not uniformly clear. The flowers were a thousand different shades, laced with small hints of colour. She reached down and picked a stem, which snapped like an icicle breaking from a window ledge. Looking closely, she saw it was translucent but run through with craggy fissures that shone gently. She realized she was holding her breath, as if she feared that the slightest change would break the spell.

There was a low cliff off to one side and, hoping to get a better view of the place, Jess turned to head in that direction. She skirted along the bottom of the rise until the path began to climb steeply, winding its way towards the summit. She was panting heavily now, clouds of breath swirling around her. At the top was an ice boulder about the height of a tall man. *The height of Doctor Stannard*, she thought, with a lancing stab of annoyance. There was a hollow on one side that formed a kind of seat. *A throne*, she told herself as she settled into it and took in the view.

The garden stretched out around her like the parkland of a country house, but glittering white and brilliant silver. A spiderweb of winding pathways criss-crossed the rolling terrain. Here and there enormous trees stood alone, sentry-like, while smaller ones clustered in groves, as if gossiping to one other. A ring of woodland skirted the edge of the garden, cradling and containing it.

Her eyes searched the landscape, hungrily taking in each detail, and she began to name the things she saw as if they were places in one of her stories. Down amongst the flower beds was a colossal tree with a crooked trunk and two branches that hung forward like a pair of arms. *The Old Man*, she thought. On the other side of the Throne a long slope of silver grass rolled elegantly downwards – the Sweep seemed to fit it well. In the real world everything you saw, everywhere you went, had already been called something by someone else. But the ice garden was undiscovered territory. *Things can be whatever I want them to be*, she thought.

Far off, at the bottom of the Sweep, an assortment of tall hedges linked up in a strange sort of pattern. Jess stood up and squinted for a better look. All at once the shapes resolved themselves and she realized what she was looking at.

'A maze,' she said out loud. *A maze!*

She laughed, suddenly and without restraint. She threw her arms out and began to spin on the spot, cackling away. Her mind raced with the billions of thoughts and sensations brought to life by this mad, impossible place she'd discovered. This place which was all hers and no one's but hers.

But then the laughter caught in her throat at the sight of something new, something she hadn't noticed. She walked to the edge of the slope. The ground there was hard and smooth, without any covering of ice-grass. But there was one patch where the wind had created a shallow snowdrift. And there, in the middle, was a footprint. She gawped: it was the footprint of a person. But that person wasn't her.

'There's someone else here,' she said weakly, and as if in answer a faint breeze swirled and wrapped itself around her.

The *Big Book of Tales* wasn't going to write itself. Just because she'd been off exploring a bizarre new world, it didn't mean she could neglect her responsibilities. Her great project. Jess picked up her favourite pen along with several sheets of paper and flicked on her desk lamp. The temptation to simply describe the events of the night before was almost overwhelming. If she could turn that pure blast of experience into carefully chosen words and phrases, then perhaps she could start to make sense of it. But that was impossible, surely? How could mere scribbles on a page help her understand something so incredible?

And there was something else stopping her – a

creeping dread that bubbled up, bile-soaked and burning, from the bottom of her stomach when she remembered that footprint. *I wasn't alone*, she thought. There was someone else there, in her own frozen paradise. Someone who might even have been watching her.

Or was there? she asked herself. Was what she'd thought of as a footprint anything of the sort? She remembered the way her own steps had looked, the pattern from the bottom of her trainers clearly stamped into the ice grass. It hadn't been like that at all – more like the indistinct mark of a bare foot in sand. And who would go without shoes in a place like the ice garden? Still, though, her skin crept and crawled at the memory.

She scanned her room for inspiration. Thick curtains blocked out any trace of the sun. She couldn't open the windows in case a gust of wind blew them out of place and so a plug-in air-conditioning unit sat in the corner by the door, whirring and burbling away. The light above her bed was encased in a silver shade which smoothed out the glare of the bulb. The walls were covered in pictures she'd printed out. They were mostly the stuff of her imagination: towering gothic castles and deep, dark woods. But here and there were snapshots of a band she liked at the moment, whose toothy smiles and perfect hair made her heart do a little jitter.

Today, though, none of it helped. The ideas refused to come and she was reduced to scrawling practice signatures across the first sheet of paper. It was important for her to have a good signature so that she could sign all those books she was going to sell. She imagined the queues of people, the little conversations, the children explaining how much her stories had meant to them. *They'll have to close the blinds in the bookshop when I come, though. Either that or I go Full Hat.* The thought landed with a sickening thud. She hated these moments, when reality took a wrecking ball to her fantasies. She was saved from having to dwell on it by the chime of the doorbell downstairs and, a few moments later, a cheery cry of '*Bonjour!*'

Although Jess took most of her lessons with her mother, there were some subjects for which they brought in outside tutors. Of these her least favourite by far was Mrs Agatha Dobson, who insisted on speaking English with a French accent, despite originally being from somewhere near Swindon.

Jess dragged herself to her feet and plodded down the stairs.

'*Bonjour*, Jessica,' said Madame, as she liked to be called.

'It's Jess, not Jessica.'

'*En français, s'il te plaît.*'

'I don't know the French for Jessica.'

Her mother cleared her throat and shot her a look.

Madame smelt as if she showered in perfume. Anyone would think she was waging a full-scale war on the natural smells of the world around her. She was swaddled in a long dress, stitched with beads that clicked and rattled as she swished through and deposited herself at the kitchen table. Jess wondered why, if she wanted everyone to think she was from France, she hadn't at least changed her last name. *D'Obson* might work. She fetched her textbook from the pile in the hall, took a final draught of fresh air, and plunged into her lesson. But over the next hour of vocabulary and verbs, no matter how hard she tried, she couldn't stop her mind drifting to the day before. To trees of sparkling silver, of course, but also to the boy in his hospital bed.

She remembered how cold his hand had been. *Maybe he'd like a story*, she thought. Something else to listen to besides the likes of Doctor Stannard droning on. Doctors liked to make everything as difficult to understand as possible, so that you wouldn't question them. That was how they kept their power. That was how they made perfectly sensible and clever people like her mother agree to whatever they suggested, even when her own daughter knew far better what suited her best. A story would give the boy a break from all that, just for a while.

'Jessica? Jessica!' Madame patted her hand on the table.

'Sorry?'

'*"Excusez-moi", s'il te plaît!*'

Jess looked down at the book. She didn't remember turning the page. On it was a photo of a weather forecaster standing by his map. What was she meant to be doing?

'Please, Jessica. It is sunny.'

'Il fait beau.'

'It is hot.'

'Il fait chaud.'

'It is cold.'

'Il fait froid.'

'It is snowing.'

'Il neige.'

Il fait froid. Il neige . . .

The boy would like a story . . . After Madame had gone Jess retreated back upstairs to try and write. She thought first about the kind of thing he might like. But that wouldn't work, of course. She had to write the thing she wanted – to give it the flavour and scent of her own imagination.

She turned to the paper and sucked in a deep breath. She had to remove the distractions. In her mind's eye she saw herself find the entrance to the ice garden, only now it was behind a pair of elaborate metal gates. She locked them tight and pocketed the key for later. Behind her was another door, this one to the boy's hospital room and she closed that too, knowing she'd be seeing it for real sometime soon. With this mental ritual completed, she was ready to write.

She began the saga of a tailor who found that all the clothes he made would fall apart as soon as anyone said the word 'oranges'. He tried different materials, different thread, even a different sewing machine, but the outcome was the same – whenever anyone in the vicinity of his work uttered that fateful word, every stitch would come unpicked and the garment would end up a heap of cloth on the floor. She wrote quickly, her red ink flowing across the page in loops and spots.

The story smelt of citrus fruit and spices. Its characters went about their days arguing and laughing with the kind of full-throated gusto you never found on a drizzle-soaked English high street. They lived their lives under a burning Middle Eastern sun. She paused. How could she describe that? How could she communicate what that *felt* like to her reader? She stared at the page, willing something, anything, to come. Her fingers gripped her pen tighter and tighter until they turned blotchy red and white. Tears pricked at her eyes and she bit down on her lip until it hurt. She couldn't get away from it. Couldn't get away from what she was, even here in her own stories.

She forced her breathing back to normal. She was in control. *It had been raining for months, and the people thought it might never end,* she wrote. That should do it.

At last it was complete, and she leant back to survey

the four pages of messy scrawl. It was short, she thought, but good.

There was a knock on the door and a moment later her mother popped her head round with eyes crossed and cheeks puffed out. Jess tried to stifle a laugh and turned it into a snort. Her mother grinned back.

'You OK, little one?' she said.

'Just finished a new one.'

'Can I read it?'

'When—' Jess started.

'The whole book's done,' her mother finished for her. 'I know, I know.' She shook her head. 'Anyway, I need you to get ready.'

'Ready for what?'

'For an outing.'

'Where are we going?'

'You'll find out when we get there.'

'Full Hat?'

'Full Hat.'

'Do we have to?' Jess winced at the whiny note in her own voice.

'Don't be like that, you don't know where we're going.'

'Is it somewhere I'll like?'

'Come on, we're going to be late.'

'Tell me,' she insisted.

'To the hospital.'

'But we went yesterday!'

‘Well, you don’t usually have a burn like that one, do you?’ Her mother nodded at the bandage on Jess’s wrist.

‘So you knew we had to go back?’

‘Doctor said we must, while you were off wandering.’

‘And you didn’t tell me!’

‘No, because I didn’t want to put up with a temper like this for twenty-four hours.’

Jess’s blood hissed like water droplets on a hotplate. She clenched her jaw and tried to burn holes in her mother’s face with the sheer power of her glare.

Her mother sighed. ‘I’m sorry, all right? I should have said. Look, I don’t like it any more than you.’ She changed tack, hardening her voice to flint. ‘Jessica, your wrist is a complete mess. It needs attention and it needs to be rebandaged. Now come on or we’ll be late.’

Jess dragged herself to her feet.

‘And I am sorry. Little one? I said I am.’

Her mother extended one hand and, after a moment, Jess linked fingers with her. Each gave a small smile, not realizing how much alike their expressions were.

As they left the room, Jess grabbed the pages of ‘The Unfortunate Tailor’ and dropped them into a plastic wallet. She would have a chance to deliver it to its audience sooner than she’d thought.

How to slip away? That was the question rattling around her brain as the nurse worked away at her burn. The wound was ugly and weeping, and the woman's plastic-gloved fingers stung, but Jess tried not to grimace.

When they were done, she trailed her mother back through the labyrinth of corridors. At this rate she'd be taking the story straight home with her again and that was no good. The boy would appreciate hearing it, she thought, even if he couldn't respond. *Think, Jess,* she told herself. She'd managed to discover a magical new world, surely she could work out how to slip away for a little while? She could come clean, of course, but her mother might think the whole thing was ridiculous, which would put an end to it before it really began. She could tell her she needed to go to the toilet, but that wouldn't give her enough time. She was all out of ideas, and they were almost at the lift, when a shrill note sounded from her mother's pocket. She answered her phone and the moment Jess heard her voice get a little deeper and a little slower she knew it was about work.

'I'm very sorry, I'm actually out at the moment. I could give you a call when I get home. Should be twenty minutes or so.'

Jess shook her head until she feared it would fall off.

What? her mother mouthed in return.

'Take the call,' she hissed. 'I'll be fine.'

Her mother pursed her lips, forming a delta of little lines around her mouth which Jess adored. *'It's fine, honestly,'* she whispered.

Her mother nodded. 'Actually, I can talk now after all.'

Jess scuttled to the boy's room, breaking into a half run when alone and slowing to a walk when anyone came by. She thought she must be a strange sight, even without the Hat. She tapped on the door and, when no answer came, poked her head inside. He was alone. Everything was the same, apart from the photo which had fallen face down. She righted it, closed the blinds, and dragged a heavy wooden chair out from the corner. Then she took off her hood.

'Hello again, sleepy boy,' she said, taking the papers

out of their plastic wallet. 'I brought you something.' She brushed a fan of light brown hair away from his forehead. His face was heart-shaped, with high, sharp cheekbones that were dotted with freckles. His eyelids showed a road map of pale veins. She settled down beside him and began to read. 'Once upon a time there was a tailor,' she started, 'whose clothes were the very best in the land. It was said that his dresses could make the plainest woman beautiful, and his suits could make princes out of the humblest men. There was only one problem, and that problem had to do with fruit . . .'

As she read the story out loud she found she could see the characters and places just as surely as she could see the real world. She told the boy about an angry greengrocer who ended up stark naked in his shop and threatened the tailor so violently he was forced to flee the city. He travelled around for years, searching for a place where no one had ever heard of oranges. Eventually he came to a small island where the soil was so poor they couldn't grow crops. The islanders ate nothing but fish. This was the place the tailor had been searching for. He opened a new shop and, though the islanders had no teeth on account of never eating fruit, and especially not oranges, they became widely acknowledged as the best-dressed folk in the whole world.

'And the tailor was happy,' she concluded, 'for all the people loved him.' Jess bowed her head. Her breathing locked in with the hiss and wheeze of the boy's own. Monitors blinked and told their stories.

'You remember what I said to you?' Jess whispered. 'About wishing there was no sun in the sky?' She tensed at the approach of voices in the corridor outside, but they passed by. 'I found somewhere,' she went on. 'I don't know how, or why, or even what it is, not really, but I found a place. And it's beautiful. My ice garden.'

She rose and picked up a card from the windowsill. Inside it read:

Davey-boy.

Stop being so lazy and wake up.

All my love, Uncle Jamie.

'Davey,' she said, tasting the word. 'Did you like the story? I can bring you another one if you like. I know you're in there, listening. And I know that you're a bit like me. You don't get to decide what happens to you either. That's why . . .' She felt foolish saying it, and yet it somehow felt correct. 'That's why we're friends. I'll come and see you again. I will. I'll bring you another story, Davey. I'll come and see you again.'

9

She hadn't imagined it. She knew she hadn't imagined it. And yet, as she crossed the playground and pushed through the fir trees, she couldn't help but fear it would somehow have been taken away from her. *Please be there,* she thought. *Please.*

Jess stepped through the gap in the hedge and into the ice garden. The summer night gave way at once to a chill that nipped at the exposed skin of her face. She thought the moment should feel *bigger* somehow. Surely as she crossed the boundary there should be a dizzying rush or a burst of light, but there was nothing of the sort. Instead, moving from one world to another was as simple and uneventful as getting off the bus.

She sucked in a draught of freezing air, inviting the

cold into her nose and lungs. It was clean and clear, as pure as crystal. The purple sky was streaked with brontosaurus ribs of white cloud.

She pulled on the winter coat she'd rescued from the back of her cupboard before sneaking out, and took her gloves from the pockets. The musty smell of damp wool floated up for a moment and was gone. She threw on a small rucksack, containing a bottle of water and a packet of chocolate biscuits. *Be Prepared*, they said in the Scouts. Jess wasn't a Scout, on account of it being largely an out-and-about-in-the-daytime kind of operation, but that didn't mean she couldn't follow good advice when she heard it.

This time she took a different trail, cutting through a rolling expanse of ice flowers. The ground was a kind of gravel: small cubes that crunched under her feet. She felt no less a sense of wonder on this second visit. If anything, she was able to see and appreciate so much more, and didn't even try to keep the grin off her face.

She was impatient to get to the woods she'd spied the day before from up by the Throne. The going wasn't too difficult, but the garden was larger than she'd realized and before long her clothes were plastered to her skin despite the cold. At last she made it, paused for a second, and then plunged inside.

All around her the white trunks were adorned with delicate silver leaves. Glowing spheres hung from the branches like coloured Christmas baubles. *It's fruit,* she realized. *Ice-apples.* The woods weren't just woods; they were an orchard! She reached up and plucked a luminous yellow ball from one of the lowest branches. She paused, knowing full well you shouldn't eat wild things you don't know for sure are safe. *Oh, well,* she thought, and took a bite.

Pain lanced through her front teeth and into her brain. *All right,* she thought, *not a good idea. Cold. Way, way too cold.* Instead she peeled away the top half of the shell to reveal a swimming pool of shining gold liquid inside. She tipped her head back and drank. There was an icy stab as it washed down her throat, but that soon transformed into a strange warmth that spread all the way through her body and out to the tips of her fingers.

She weaved through the trees, selecting more pieces of fruit, cracking them open and dipping a finger in to taste. The deep blues were tangy and sharp, while the reds smacked almost of liquorice. Before long she had a sticky mouth and churning stomach. She let out a vast burp that eased the pressure a little and made her laugh. *Imagine burping in front of Madame D'Obson or Doctor Stannard.*

A gentle breeze began to blow. It caught on the edges of the ice-leaves, making them sing. They whistled softly, like the sound of a wet finger being dragged round the edge of a glass.

There came a sudden rustling sound from the undergrowth. Jess jumped back, alarmed. Then a whiskered nose peeked out from under a broad leaf. It was followed by a fat, furry body on which every strand of hair was made of glistening frost. The animal was the size and shape of a mouse but with floppy ears that were far too large and dragged along the ground. Its sapphire blue eyes locked on to her.

'Hello,' she said. The creature sniffed the air, taking in her unfamiliar smell. 'What are you then, little one?' she asked. But in the ice garden nothing had a name until she gave it one. 'Elephant Mouse,' she said. 'I hereby name your species the Elephant Mouse.' The animal gave a small squeak, as if agreeing, and Jess giggled with excitement.

It began to sniff around and eventually settled by an ice-apple that lay shattered and pooled on the ground. The liquid had already frozen and the mouse started to nibble at it, chiselling away with needle-sharp front teeth. Jess broke off a piece of the fruit she was carrying and, very slowly, placed it on the ground. She did the same with a few more chunks until there was a trail for the little animal to follow. She took a few steps back and waited.

The creature's head jerked up as it caught a whiff of the still-liquid nectar oozing on to the woodland floor. Without taking its eyes off her for a second, it shuffled forward, ears dragging on the ground, and gobbled up the first piece of fruit. On it came, unable to help itself, taking each bit in turn until it came to a stop right next to Jess's foot. This was the moment of truth. She barely dared to breathe as she slipped one of her gloves off and reached down. The mouse's fur stood up on end. Cold jolted through her fingers as they made the briefest contact, and to her dismay the creature broke into a scurrying, weaving run away from her.

'No!' said Jess, jumping up. 'I don't want to hurt you! Stupid thing!'

The Elephant Mouse made it to the edge of a sharp embankment and launched itself into the air. A pair of delicate, dragonfly wings unfolded from its back and it spread its ears wide so that it could glide safely to the ground. Jess cried out in delight. 'You're a Flying Elephant Mouse!' she shouted, and scrambled down the slope after it.

She raced through the trees, catching glimpses of the creature as it burrowed and darted ahead of her. She laughed as she ran, flinging herself around corners and leaping over roots.

Then all of a sudden the ground disappeared and Jess came skidding to a halt on the lip of an enormous crevasse. Her feet went from under her and she tumbled over on to the diamond-hard ice, driving all the breath from her body. She flopped on to her back, gasping and staring up at a blanket of purple sky.

She pulled herself to her feet. In front of her there was a chasm at least a hundred metres wide, stretching in both directions to form a moat around the entire garden. She peered into the pit but the bottom was hidden in darkness. She picked up an ice rock, threw it in, and listened. No sound came back. If she'd gone over the edge, how long would she have fallen for? *For ever*, she thought, skin crawling.

There was a narrow frost bridge spanning the drop. It looked no firmer than the icing on a cake. A curved handrail ran along one side but crumbled away to nothing halfway across. On the far side a path led into a deep forest. Its mass of trunks, branches and vines twisted and coiled around each other. The ice, so bright and beautiful within the garden, looked dark and forbidding there. She shuddered.

A thought came, uninvited. How can there be a bridge? Bridges are built by people. But then gardens are built by people too . . .

Her thoughts were interrupted by a high-pitched beeping sound from her wrist. *So soon?* On her first visit Jess had been disappointed to learn that, unlike the magical realms she'd read about in books, time ran just as quickly in the ice garden as it did everywhere else. She had half expected that she could spend as long as she liked there and return to the real world to find only a few minutes had passed. This, annoyingly, wasn't the case. She'd got home to find it was almost morning and so, this time, had made sure to set an alarm.

As she turned away she caught a glimpse of something moving ahead of her. Or did she? Had there been a shape, there, running through the trees? She glanced back at the bridge. If there really was something in the orchard with her, then that might be her only escape. But on the other side was the forest . . . *There's no way I'm going there*, she thought.

There it was again! She was sure this time. A ripple of darkness behind the ice trunks and a sharp snapping noise. Her heart began to hammer out a frantic rhythm in her chest.

'Hello?' she said in a weak voice.

Fruit falling? A tree creaking? If you pour water on to ice, you hear it spit and crack inside – perhaps it was something like that.

Or someone stepping on a branch, she thought.

Jess started back towards the heart of the garden, sure now that she was being watched. The cold had seeped into her bones and she shivered, hunching her shoulders. Constantly checking from side to side, she hurried on through the trees. Terror bubbled inside her, threatening to boil over. At last she made it back out into the open. From the top of the rise she could see the wall, rearing up into the purple sky and there, in the centre of it, the thin crack leading back to her own world. It seemed far away, surely further than she'd walked. Had the garden grown bigger or was her mind playing tricks? There was only one thing for it.

She ran.

She ran madly, full of fear. She ran down the slope, along the main path, winding through the flower beds and not stopping until she reached the gap. She rested her hand on it, feeling the laurel branches prick the cold skin of her palm. Real leaves, not ice. She looked back. The garden was as pristine and still as ever.

But, she saw – stomach lurching – it wasn't empty.

There was a dark figure standing on the brow of the distant hill. She was right. Someone had been watching her all along.

10

The next day was like a held breath. A suffocating blanket of heat descended on the town. In Jess's house the mercury crept ever upward and, at last, her mother had no choice but to throw open the windows and most of the curtains. 'We have to get some air running through,' she said, 'before we both roast.' Jess was trapped in even fewer rooms than usual. She tugged at her collar and fanned herself as best she could with the *Big Book of Tales*.

She did her lessons, as always. Today there was maths, history and geography. Triangles, Vikings and oxbow lakes. Her mother was distracted, repeatedly pausing to dab away the moisture that pooled at her throat. 'Can't wait until Christmas,' she said at last.

'Can we get a real tree this year?' asked Jess.

'As long as it's cooler, you can get what you like.'

After sandwiches for lunch, her mother settled down at the kitchen table. She worked for a copywriting agency who produced leaflets, brochures and manuals for their clients. Her job was to take whatever splurge of words she'd been presented with and turn it into something that someone might actually want to read. Today she was writing a leaflet that would be given to every new employee of a big bank. *Welcome to the family!* it proclaimed. The work made her brain dribble from her ears, she sometimes said.

Jess went upstairs to do some writing of her own, but again no ideas came. Her pen nib rested on the paper, idle. A small circle of red ink soaked through the fibres and spread outwards. *For Davey*, she told herself. Davey, stuck in his hospital bed, who desperately needed to be taken away to some strange and magical world. She could do that for him. She just had to write a story.

She created a bare, white room in her mind, with an entrance in each wall. Usually when she did this, someone or other would come in through one of the doors. They might be carrying something with them, or be dressed in a certain way. Once she had two people, they would almost certainly start to speak. Before long the white room would warp and change into something else. A story would begin. But today no one came.

Instead, her mind rolled back to the night before.

She'd hurried home through town, her skin tingling. Someone else had found *her* place. Who were they? What did they want?

It *was* her garden, wasn't it? She felt colour rise in her cheeks. Other people had a whole world to play in – a world that she would never enjoy. How dare one of them come wandering in like that? And how dare she run? How dare she give up ground so easily? As if she were the intruder, not them.

But she'd been frightened, and that was what stuck in her throat more than anything. Frightened. Frightened, like the night she'd run away from shadows in the playground, like the moment she'd looked over the chasm at the ice forest, like each and every time she went into hospital. Maybe she didn't deserve the ice garden. Perhaps the stranger had come to tell her that she couldn't visit any more.

Her thoughts were pebbles thrown into a pool. They sent ripples through her mind and came to rest on the bottom, heavy and unwelcome.

'Jess!' came a shout from downstairs, and she heard the sound of curtain rings scraping on poles. 'Full Hat please, now.'

Being in the Hat was like being in a portable oven. They hurried to the other end of the road, where their car was squeezed in, nose to tail, amongst their neighbours' vehicles.

Once safely inside, Jess pulled off the hood. The engine coughed for a moment before settling into a throaty, contented rumble. Her mother pressed the button for air conditioning and turned the dial to full. Moments later a delicious stream of cool breeze began to snake through the car's interior. Jess sat back in her seat and sighed.

'I couldn't stay in that house a moment longer,' her mother said at last.

The two of them sat side by side, relishing every tiny drop in temperature until they were genuinely cool for the first time that day. Her mother moved to turn the air conditioning down but Jess lightly touched her outstretched hand and shook her head. The cold air felt a little like standing at the top of the Sweep in the face of an ice-edged breeze.

'Well, we can't sit here all day,' her mother said at last. She knocked the car into gear and see-sawed back and forth until they were clear of their space. The town centre was almost deserted. They rolled over endless speed bumps while a stream of chatter poured from the radio. Out of town they went, past the clusters of corrugated metal warehouses, past office buildings, past the gleaming retail park with its vast supermarket and clothes stores.

'I love this one!' her mother shouted and ratcheted up the volume. She began to sing along, missing as many notes as she hit. Jess couldn't help but giggle and soon the two of them were in fits, so much so they had to pull over for a while.

The countryside opened up around them. Little hedges crowded the lanes. Behind them fields overflowed with golden stalks coming to their full height. A heady scent of pollen was sucked through the air conditioning and dispersed into the cabin. But it was all in shadow, of course, as if seen from behind sunglasses. The specially tinted windows took care of that.

They traced a large and meandering circle to re-enter town from the other side. The houses were large there – grand things hiding away behind their automatic gates.

Jess recognized the route. She leant forward in her seat and sure enough her mother swung the car on to Weston Road. The engine grumbled as they started up the steep hill and Jess turned her head towards the park. There were a few people on the grass, some shaded by large beech trees, others lying under the full face of the sun. The playground was all but empty, just a solitary woman pushing a little boy on the swing. She was grateful not to see more children playing. Grateful she didn't have to feel jealous.

They came to a halt at a pedestrian crossing part way up the hill. Jess almost gasped. From here she had a perfect view down on to the conifers ringing the playground and the laurel hedge behind them. She could see the gap that led into the ice garden. It looked so small, so unremarkable. On the other side of it was a pockmarked football pitch, sketched out in tired white paint. Who would have thought that it was the route to another world? The world of ice-apples, the Old Man and the Flying Elephant Mouse! The world only she had seen!

Her thoughts derailed and mangled. *The stranger.* The stranger had seen it too.

They pulled up at a set of traffic lights outside the hospital. Jess stiffened a little and glanced at her mother. 'Don't worry,' she sighed, 'we're not going in. This wasn't all some plot to get you here.'

'But can we?' The words were out before Jess had a chance to decide if she wanted to say them or not.

'Can we what?'

'Go in.'

'You *want* to go to hospital today?' The lights went green and her mother pulled the car up on to the kerb. 'Usually I have to drag you kicking and screaming.'

'That's an exaggeration.'

'Why would we go in? We don't have an appointment.' Dark clouds of concern scudded across her mother's face. 'Unless . . . is it your burn? Is it worse?'

'There's a boy,' Jess blurted. Her mother's jaw opened but no words came out. 'I mean, I met a boy.'

'You did? Right. I mean. Well, I wasn't expecting . . . You met a boy.'

'Well, not really met.'

'No?'

'He's asleep.'

'Right.'

'Unconscious, I mean. He's a patient. I found his room sort of by accident.'

'And when exactly did you sort of by accident do this?'

'Two days ago. And then yesterday I read him one of my stories. He liked it, I think. Though obviously he can't really say.'

'Because he's unconscious.'

'That's right.'

Her mother had the look of someone who has been completely left behind.

'So?'

'So what?'

'Can I go and visit him?'

'Jess, you can't just go wandering into other patient's rooms!'

Jess felt her skin prickle. *Other patients.* She was a patient, even to her mother.

'I just want to see how he is. We're right here. I read about it – it's good for people like him.'

'What is?'

'To be talked to.'

'I'm sure he has plenty of family to talk to him.'

'But they don't have stories like mine.'

Her mother frowned. 'I could ask Doctor Stannard, I suppose . . .'

'No!' It was almost a shout. 'No,' she said more gently, 'we don't need to do that. It's fine. We don't need to ask his permission for everything, do we?'

They pulled away and for a moment Jess thought her pleading had been in vain, but a second later they swung into the car park.

'Hello, Davey,' said Jess. Her mother had agreed she could pop her head in for a few minutes. 'The Unfortunate Tailor' was still on the table by the bed, she noticed with pleasure. She would have to write a new story as soon as she could. She went to fetch the chair but just then the door squeaked open and a woman came in. Jess recognized her at once from the photo. She looked almost as different to the holiday snap as the boy did, though. The laughter had died and vivid purple bags hung under her eyes.

'What are you—?' she started. Her voice was high and reedy. 'You're not supposed to be in here.'

'I'm sorry,' said Jess, grabbing her hood to her chest. Neither of them moved.

'You're not meant to be in here,' the woman said again. Her accent was soft and lilting.

'I came to see Davey. To see how he was.'

'How do you know Davey? He doesn't know anyone around here, we only moved just before . . . just before.' Her eyes darted to her son, lying in the bed.

'I brought him a story yesterday,' Jess explained, and immediately felt foolish. 'I have to come for appointments here, you see.'

The woman's eyes flickered in half recognition and then all at once a smile cracked open, like sunlight breaking through cloud. *She's beautiful*, thought Jess.

'It's *you*!' said the boy's mother. 'You're the one! I came in yesterday and saw it there. I didn't know where it could have come from.'

'I read it to him,' Jess said. 'I thought he might hear it.'

'Yes! He does!' The woman was nodding vigorously now. 'I'm sure of it. He hears everything. "The Unfortunate Tailor", is it?' she went on. 'I liked it. Thought it was very good.'

'Is he . . . is Davey . . . is he getting any better?'

For a moment the woman looked unsteady on her feet and Jess feared that she would cry, but she mastered herself and shook her head. 'No. The doctors don't think . . . well, they think he might never . . .' She stopped, unable to continue.

Jess felt a great wave of sympathy and pain rise up through her chest. 'If you want to know what I think, it's that doctors don't know as much as they say.'

'No?'

'No. They're always telling me that I can't do something, but half the time I think they're just doing it to be difficult. I told my mum that and she said *I'm* difficult sometimes, but she doesn't mean it because I'm actually a delight.'

The woman was about to reply but at that moment Jess's mother appeared at the door. 'I couldn't find Doctor and I . . .' Seeing her daughter had company, she swallowed her words mid-sentence and shifted from one foot to the other. 'I'm sorry,' she said at last, in the absence of anything else to explain the presence of two strangers in the room.

'That's OK,' the woman replied. Then, 'Your daughter's very talented.'

Jess's mother stopped for a second and a little smile tugged at the corners of her mouth. 'It's very nice to meet you,' she said. 'And I'm so terribly sorry about your son.'

Davey's mother bobbed her head.

'Come on, little one, time to go,' said Jess's mum.

As they left the room the woman called out, 'You'll write more, won't you? Promise me you will? I'm sure he likes hearing them.'

Jess nodded, then paused a moment. 'I think he'll wake up soon,' she said.

'Well, then, we'll keep our fingers crossed, you and I.'

'Full Hat, Jessica. Now, please,' said her mother. She sounded stern, but on the way down she put an arm around Jess's shoulder and didn't stop squeezing until the doors had opened to the foyer.

The tension that had built all day broke just before the sun went down. Heavy clouds bullied their way across the sky, locking arms and casting the day into premature darkness. They paused for a second to gather their strength then tore themselves open, hurling great sheets of rain on to the streets below. It bounced up ankle-high from the tarmac. A violent, gusting wind rampaged around the town.

It was dark enough that Jess could open the curtains and look out, although she still sat back from the window. There was something beautiful about it. Something fierce and strong. A man skittered down the road, struggling to stay upright in the gale. He held a blown-out umbrella above his head. *Causes more problems than it solves*, Jess thought. Lamps flickered to life all along the street.

Every now and then flashes of light would tickle her eyes and she'd count the seconds – one, two, three, four, five – until there came a report of distant thunder. It would get louder, the number of seconds dropping fast, until the flash and sound were almost together and the lightning was right above them. Then it would move off until the next wave came.

They ate in near silence, conversation and radio replaced by the booming and hammering of the storm.

'You're not scared, are you?' her mother asked her later, as Jess started up the stairs towards bed.

She curled her lip and snorted but didn't feel as certain as she seemed.

'You used to come running into my room, you know. Come jumping right into bed with me. Every time there was a storm.'

'I remember,' said Jess. And then, after a pause, 'I don't think I'll need to do that tonight.'

Her mother smiled a small smile. 'No, I don't suppose you will.'

She climbed a few more stairs.

'You know, the first time you saw fireworks . . .' her mother called. 'You were scared out of your wits. Kept asking if they'd fall on you.' She gave that little half-smile once more and Jess turned towards bed.

The wind continued its banshee howl but the rain eventually stopped. Jess was relieved – she hadn't fancied exploring the ice garden while completely soaked through.

Later, there were footsteps on the staircase and in time the light under the door went out. Minutes went by and then Jess climbed out of bed.

She was halfway into her clothes when an almighty clap of thunder rattled the windows. Seconds later a light came back on. Jess scrabbled at her clothing, tearing off what she could while a shadow moved across the hallway towards her. She jumped under the covers, taking her bundled clothes with her and hoping they weren't obvious.

Her mother knocked twice and the door swung open. Jess blinked, as if just waking from a deep sleep.

'Are you OK?' she was asked.

'Of course.' Jess yawned and stretched. *Don't overdo it!*

'I thought . . . I thought you might be frightened. That was a big one.'

'Big one what?'

'The thunder! You didn't hear?'

'I wondered what woke me up.'

'Deep sleeper, like your mother.'

'Don't worry, I wasn't scared.'

Something stabbed at Jess's heart and turned a little. 'Thanks for looking in on me,' she said. Her mother smiled. A proper one this time.

'Night, little one.'

'Night, Mum.'

It was only when she was sure her mother was safely returned to her own room that Jess let out a long juddering breath.

That was close, she thought. Too close.

She waited for half an hour, and then made her way out into the gale.

12

It was an almost physical relief to step through the gap once more, like coming up for a lungful of air. And yet all at once a sense of dread came creeping up on Jess, a whispering worry about the stranger she'd seen watching from the woods.

Her imagination had always been her best friend. She had trained it – honed it to be as powerful as it possibly could be, to feel as real as it possibly could feel. But it wasn't real. Not real in the way this place was. This strange place. This empty place. This place with its purple sky that didn't burn her skin. *Her place.* And now it had been invaded. There was nothing for it but to find the stranger. To find answers to the questions suddenly running wild inside her. With an effort, she pushed her fears to one side and went forward.

She took a small trail through the great beds of Snowbuds and Frostblossom – naming them as she went – until she came to a mass of high, white bushes. The vegetation formed a long wall, in the centre of which was the entrance to the Maze.

She made her way cautiously, rounding two sharp corners first left and then right. The hedges on either side were at least three times her height. Their branches were twisted and tangled, each one adorned with hundreds of silver-blue leaves. Here and there hung groups of blood-red ice-berries. But the strangest thing was that the paths were completely clear, as if the bushes had been deliberately pruned back. *Pruned by who?* she thought. What if the stranger wasn't an intruder from her world at all? What if it was the person who tended the garden?

After a few more turns she came to a junction that led off in three directions. She paused. After all, a child alone probably *shouldn't* enter a labyrinth. But, given that she was already hopping back and forth between two worlds, she decided she could probably just about manage it. Besides, her footprints in the snow would show her the way out again.

As she went deeper the bushes reached over at the top to form a high arch. The sky was obscured and every step took her further into inky darkness. Chills raced down her spine, and she walked more and more slowly until she finally came to a stop.

What on earth are you doing, Jessica? she heard her mother ask inside her head. *This is very silly and very risky, don't you think?*

'I don't mind taking risks,' Jess replied to her imaginary parent. 'Do you know how boring it is for me every day?'

We've talked about this, darling, she heard her mother say. *Things are what they are. And you've lots to be thankful for. So why don't you turn round, come home and get back into bed?*

'I'll be back as soon as I find out who's been visiting my garden.'

And how will you do that?

'I'll keep looking.'

You could get lost. You could fall and be hurt. There's no one around to help you.

'I won't get lost.'

Don't forget, I'll be waking up soon.

'I know.'

If I'm not awake already. Her mother's voice became a flickering fork-tongued hiss. *I'm awake right now, Jessica, I've walked into your room and found that my daughter has been turned into a clumsy pile of pillows. My heart is shattering, darling, breaking into pieces all over your bedroom floor . . .*

Jess shut the door on the voice and locked it tight. That wasn't her mother; it was her own guilt slithering and coiling around her brain. But what choice did she have? Without the garden, she'd be reduced once more to her stories and to conjuring up phantom friends in a deserted playground.

She forced herself to go deeper into the Maze, choosing turnings whenever it felt the right thing to do. On she went, trying to focus on nothing but where she was, what she was doing at that very moment.

She rounded a corner and all at once the breath left her body.

Standing at the end of the passage was a figure.

A boy.

A boy made of ice, shining blue and white.

'Who are you?' he said. 'What are you doing here?'

13

Jess felt as if she'd stood up too quickly from a hot bath. Her head swam. *He's made of ice*, she thought. The stranger wasn't from her world after all. His eyes were blue jewels under lashes of glistening frost. His body was an intricate web of interconnecting icicles. But despite all that, he was undoubtedly a boy, of about her height and age. *And he's barefoot*, she noticed. It *had* been a footprint that she'd seen.

'I said, what are you doing here?' he tried again, voice rising. She noticed flurries of snow that swirled and whipped around his feet in time with his angry words. 'What are you doing in my garden? You don't belong here.'

She couldn't help but flinch. His garden – not hers. Not a sanctuary after all.

'I'm talking to you!' he called, and an icy blast of wind suddenly rattled through the Maze.

'I'm not doing anything wrong,' she protested, taking a few paces back in case the boy was dangerous.

'You're in my garden,' he snapped, eyes glittering with anger.

'I know,' she said.

'Why are you in my garden?'

'I found it.'

'Found it how?'

'I don't know, I just found it. I didn't think there was anyone here.' She could hear the defensive whine in her voice.

'I saw you in the woods.'

'I thought so,' she replied.

'So you *did* know someone was here, then,' he said, in triumph.

'Well, yes, I suppose. But I meant at first. I didn't know there was anyone here at first. And then I realized there was.'

'And you still came back.'

She noticed the boy's fingers were trembling. He was scared too. He was scared of *her*. She took a step towards him.

'Don't try anything!' he barked, and the snow in front of him whirled up into a small tornado, no more than shin-high, that skittered towards her before breaking apart.

She held both palms up in a gesture of peace.

'Just stay where you are,' he said.

'All right,' she agreed. 'My name's Jess.'

The boy considered this. 'You're not made of ice,' he said at last.

'No.'

'How's that possible?'

'Well, because I'm a girl.'

'And girls aren't made of ice?'

'No, but boys aren't either. No one is.' Jess felt her fear start to ebb away.

'I'm a boy and I'm made of ice.'

'I meant no one is where I come from.'

'And where's that?'

From the real world, she thought. 'Through the crack in the wall.'

'You found that?'

'Well, yes.'

'You found the opening?'

'I mean – it wasn't on purpose. I just stepped through a gap and here I was.'

The boy seemed to relax just a little at that, as if something suddenly made sense. 'And if no one's made of ice where you come from, then what are they made of?' he asked.

'Of normal stuff. You know, skin and bone and muscle and things.'

He shuddered. 'I don't know what any of that is, but

it all sounds disgusting.'

Jess smiled. 'I suppose it is, in a way.' She took another step towards him.

'Don't try anything,' he said again, but with rather less conviction than before.

'Try anything like what?'

'Anything bad.'

'Why would I do that?'

The boy frowned and shook his head. 'I don't know,' he admitted.

He looked so small and fierce that Jess couldn't help but laugh.

'What?' he demanded.

'Nothing, just . . . You're not what I was expecting.'

'Well, what were you expecting?'

It was Jess's turn to admit she didn't know.

'Then how can I not be it?'

The boy had a point, but Jess wasn't about to concede that. 'What's your name?' she asked. 'I mean – do you have a name?'

'Of course I do. It's Owen,' he said.

'Well, it's nice to meet you, Owen.'

'It's nice to meet you too.' He set his face. 'As long as you're not an enemy, I mean.'

'I'm not an enemy.'

'Right, but you'd be a pretty stupid kind of enemy to just come out and admit you were an enemy, wouldn't you?'

'I think if I was an enemy, I'd be the kind who goes around shouting about how awful I was so that everyone would be afraid of me.'

'Well, that makes me feel a bit better, then.' A shy grin flickered across the boy's face and she saw that his teeth were like rows of delicate needles.

'Your garden's beautiful,' she told him.

The fissures deep inside Owen's body glowed red for a moment, like blown coal.

'I mean, I haven't seen much of it. I've had a little look around. I saw quite a lot from up at the Throne.'

'The what?'

'The Throne. That's what I call that big chair-like ice cube up on the hill. I suppose you've got your own names for things, though, haven't you?'

'No, not really.'

'So how does that work? Like, how do you explain where you'll be?'

'Explain to whom?'

'To the others.'

'What others? I'm the only one here.'

Alone, thought Jess. *All alone*.

'Do you want to see something good?' the boy asked, brightly, all his earlier anger and suspicion now gone.

'What?'

He smiled again. 'I'll show you,' he said, and held out his hand. As Jess took it she jerked backwards from the fierce cold that jolted into her like an electric shock, even through the thick wool of her gloves.

But Owen had already spun on his heel and dashed away. She set off and careered through the Maze after him, heart hammering in her chest with the effort of keeping pace. He was impossibly sure-footed. While she skidded and slipped like a baby deer, he never once stumbled. He kept just ahead of her, glancing back now and then with a broad smile plastered over his face. 'Keep up!' he shouted, laughing.

Jess found herself giggling as she ran – two activities that make each other more difficult but are none the worse for it. She was doing it. She was really doing it. She was playing outside with another child. Before long the two of them were in fits, gasping for breath as they went. When Owen laughed, he glowed from within. It was like the final moments of sunset – colours catching, flaming and dying away.

'Where are we going?' Jess called. 'Do you even know the way?'

It didn't make any sense. The Maze hadn't looked all that large when seen from the Throne. Yet here she was, hurtling around corner after corner, further and further, never along the same trail twice, as if she was in a vast labyrinth that covered the entire garden.

'How big is this place?' she shouted, and heard a bark of laughter from her companion as he vanished from sight.

Her breath was ragged and the smell of blood caught

in her nose. 'Owen?' she said. Then louder, 'Owen!' She rounded a corner and there were suddenly thousands of passages to choose from, far more than should have been able to fit into such a small space. Each of them led into darkness, gaping like the mouths of some many-headed creature. She was panting, drenched in sweat, laughing no more. *This is impossible*, she thought.

There was a rushing sound that might have been coming from inside her head. She could swear that shadows were leaking from the tunnels in front, spilling across the ground towards her feet. The blackness was deep and rich and hungry. She took a few steps back. *Don't let it touch me. Please, don't let it touch me.* She thought she heard a voice, speaking to her from the dark. *What are you?* The words were in her head, hissing and spitting, but they weren't her thoughts. *What are you, girl?*

She stumbled backwards and to her horror found that the hedges had closed up behind her, blocking off her escape. The blackness snaked closer and closer. It was almost at her toes. She closed her eyes.

Nothing.

Her lids fluttered open and there was just one passage left, curving gently away in front of her. She took a few steps forward, half expecting some shadowy limb to dart out and grab her. But none came. The path led her out of the Maze and on to the top of a sharp rise. Owen was there, leaning against a tree.

'What was that?' Her voice cracked in her dry throat.

'What do you mean?'

'What did you do?'

'Nothing!'

'That wasn't normal. That wasn't like anything else that's happened here. That wasn't . . .' She couldn't find the words. She blinked away the tears that threatened to come. *Stop it, Jess,* she told herself.

'What are you talking about?' he said. 'I was waiting. What took you so long?'

She searched his face for signs of a lie. 'Then you didn't do that? It wasn't you?'

'What wasn't me?'

'There was something . . .' she said. 'It was coming for me.'

'There's nothing in there. Just hedges.' Owen frowned.

'And the Maze,' she went on, 'it was different. Larger. Much larger than I thought. How can that be?'

'The garden's bigger than it looks, Jess.'

'What do you mean?'

'It has layers,' he said, opening his arms. 'It unfolds. At least, it does for me.'

She sat down heavily, her legs aching. Was it true? She realized how little she really knew the garden. She wasn't like this boy of ice.

'How long have you been here, Owen?' she asked.

He didn't answer. Instead he turned and pointed. 'Look,' he said, 'this is what I wanted you to see.'

She caught sight of it at once – a steep, smooth groove that snaked down the hillside to the garden below. 'It's a slide,' she said, delighted. In the open, under the gentle sky, the darkness of the Maze felt far away.

Owen went first, turning to give a last piece of advice. 'Make sure you lift your legs when you get to the bottom,' he said.

As he hurtled down she thought of all the girls who went to normal schools and lived normal lives who would never in a million years do something as ridiculous as this. And she thanked her lucky stars that she'd never be normal.

Jess launched herself over the edge and flew down on her bottom, her body flung from side to side like a doll in the hands of a toddler as she sped round the bends. Something caught her eye as she went, moving in the sky above her. It was a fat, fluttering creature with its ears stretched wide. *My Flying Elephant Mouse!* she thought, and screamed with delight. She'd have to give him a name!

All of a sudden she saw the ground rushing up at her, lifted her legs just in time, and was propelled, spinning, across the ground until she came to an almost dignified halt.

'Perfect landing,' she said.

'Not bad for a first time,' corrected Owen.

Jess picked herself up. 'Shall we do it again?'

14

The next three days went by in a blur. Each day she suffered in the suffocating summer heat and every night she wrapped herself in the cooling breeze of the ice garden. More than once her mother asked if everything was all right and she had to say yes, even though that was a lie. Because things weren't all right. They were wonderful. She couldn't concentrate on her lessons or the pile of books stacked up by her bed. She had no interest in what was on television, or in playing cards. She didn't even want to make up stories, which had been her favourite thing to do for as long as she'd had favourite things. Every time she sat down to write, her mind would wander to her new friend, and all other thoughts scattered like a startled flock of birds.

Apart from the ice garden, only Davey held her attention, and she had no way of seeing him until her next hospital visit.

'What do you do, when I'm not here?' Jess asked on the second evening.

'Normal stuff,' Owen replied.

'What's normal for an ice boy?' she said.

'I sleep, I eat, I play, I think. Normal stuff.' He paused for a second. 'What do you do when you're not here?'

'Sort of the same,' she said. 'And I have lessons.'

'What are lessons?'

'Where I learn things.'

'What kind of things?'

'Things about the world,' she said.

Owen considered this. 'Don't think I need lessons,' he said at last.

'Everyone needs lessons.'

'But I already know everything I need.'

'That's silly. You can't.'

Owen shrugged. 'What did you learn today?' he asked.

'Well . . .' She took a breath. 'First of all I had maths, but my teacher couldn't come because he was in bed with the flu so Mum and I did it together instead, but I don't really think she knew what she was talking about. Then I read a book about the Industrial Revolution.'

'What's the Industrial—' started Owen.

'It's when everyone went from being farmers to working in factories and building machines and those kind of things and, I think, is probably when all the really interesting animals, like unicorns and dragons, were killed off.'

'Right,' he said, slowly.

'And then I had my French lesson.'

'What's French?'

'It's what people in France speak,' she replied.

'Is France made of ice?'

'Of course it's not. It's made of plastic, just like England.'

'I suppose I'll never go to France either, then,' he said.

'I suppose not,' she replied.

Owen looked so utterly crushed Jess didn't know whether to fling her arms around him or burst out laughing.

'What?' he asked, pouting.

'You live *here*,' she said. 'I mean, look at this place. It's amazing. You've got ice-apples! You've got Flying Elephant Mice! My world's nothing like this. It's just . . . just *normal*. There's nothing interesting at all. If I lived where you live, I'd never want to go anywhere else.'

But that wasn't true, she realized, even as the words left her mouth. Her world had jungles and mountains, and deserts that went on for hundreds of miles. It had weird little creatures with lights dangling from their heads that lived in the pitch-black at the bottom of the sea. She realized how strange the idea of an ocean would be to Owen, who'd never seen liquid water. Now she thought about it, even her little, nothingy town was something quite remarkable. It was full of people wandering around with all sorts of technology that they barely even thought about any more. It had the bizarre Madame Dobson, and Mr Olmos, with all his strange ideas. It had Davey, who somehow managed to be interesting despite the fact he was asleep the whole time! And of course it had her mother . . . All at once there was a hard lump in her throat.

A high chirping erupted from Jess's wrist. Three quick beeps followed by a pause and then three more. Owen groaned.

'I'm sorry,' she said, shutting off her alarm and clambering to her feet. 'Time's up.'

She didn't try and write a story the next day. Instead, as soon as she'd finished a lesson on the history of canals with her mother, she got into the Hat and went across the road.

When Mr Olmos answered the door to number thirty-three, Jess was alarmed to see him brandishing a large rolling pin in one hand. But, at the sight of her, the storm clouds lifted from his face and a toothy smile broke through.

'Jessica!' he exclaimed, moving aside and waving her

past with the pin, like a policeman directing traffic. 'You haven't been round for a few days.'

'What are you doing with that?' she asked as she stepped inside.

'What, this? Nothing . . .' he said, not meeting her eye.

'You were waiting for the postman, weren't you?'

'Postman? Ha!' He pretended to spit. 'He *says* he's a postman, but is he really?'

'Well, he walks around with a big bag of post.'

'Which is clever, I agree. But you want my opinion – he's not so much a postman as a demon.' He caught Jess's sceptical look. 'A demon sent here to torment me by refusing to deliver my new apiary.'

'Your what?'

'A beehive! I'm going to start tending bees! Or at least I will as soon as that devil brings the things I've paid for fair and square. Fair and square, Jess!'

'So you were going to hit him with a rolling pin?'

'Well . . . I probably wouldn't have hit him. Just, I don't know, waved it around a bit.'

As they spoke, Jess followed her neighbour through the lounge and into an airy kitchen at the back. As ever, she felt a thrill of excitement at being at Mr Olmos's. Whereas her house was always kept neat and tidy, number thirty-three was a scene of unfettered chaos. Which is not to say it was dirty – not in the slightest. It was just that the remnants of half-completed projects lay on every table and were tucked away in the corners of rooms. There were bookshelves everywhere, bowing in the middle under the weight of their passengers. There was every type of tome imaginable, from leather-bound hardbacks that weighed half as much as she did, to yellowing old comic books. This was the perfect place to find a selection of things that would give Owen a taste of her world.

Mr Olmos pulled the blinds shut as they went. 'You can take that silly thing off your head now,' he said. 'Honestly, you look ridiculous – I don't know why you insist on wearing it.'

Jess grinned. Most adults were too freaked out by the Hat to risk making jokes.

She watched as he poured boiling water into a mug containing a bizarre-looking selection of leaves and herbs. Within seconds an evil smell floated up on the steam that rose from the cup. 'You want some?' Mr Olmos asked, offering it to her. She screwed up her face.

'Suit yourself,' he answered with a shrug.

'What is it?'

'This is what keeps me looking so young.'

Jess considered this. Mr Olmos's skin was the colour and texture of a walnut. His hair and beard were frizzy and greying. But his brown eyes were sharp, and hard and present.

'My special recipe,' he said and took a sip. 'Tastes awful, but that's not the point.' Another sip. 'But, my word, that really is terrible.'

They chatted about the upcoming bee project for a little while until Jess explained that she'd like to borrow a few things.

'What kind of things?'

'Just things. You know, random things.'

'Nothing here is random, Jessica, it just looks that way.'

'I have a friend. He's from . . . from somewhere else. I want to show what life here's like.'

'Where's he from? Is he from where I'm from? If he is, you should bring him round.'

'I don't think so, exactly, no.'

'Well, you should bring him round anyway.'

'I'm not sure that would work.' She waited. 'I'll bring everything back.'

He regarded her for a few moments. She thought he was about to ask another question but eventually he shrugged. 'Keep it all,' he said. 'My gift to you.'

At that moment they both heard the sharp clatter of the letter box and Jess dived for the rolling pin before Mr Olmos could retrieve it.

15

That night she filled her rucksack with the items she'd selected. Amongst them were an atlas, so that she could show Owen her whole world, and a book about Africa, for him to learn about some flesh-and-blood animals. There was a simple circuit board with a light attached, to show him technology, and a plastic model of an old fighter plane to explain that it wasn't always used for good. And there was a French flag, carefully folded up. If he couldn't visit France, then she'd have to bring it to him.

Finally, she opened her sock drawer and rummaged around until her fingers closed around a jewellery box. She fished it out and retrieved a small parcel of tissue paper from within. Her fingers could just about make out the shape of the object wrapped up inside. This was the most important item – the one that would show Owen a little bit more of herself. She tucked it in her pocket and made her way out.

'Thank you for my presents,' said Owen.

'*En français, s'il te plaît.*'

He looked blank.

'*Merci*,' she said. 'You say, *merci*.'

'Mercy,' he replied.

'We can work on that.'

They'd hung the flag from the branches of the Old Man. It looked strange there, dangling from the twisted ice oak. Every now and then a light breeze came waltzing through, sending ripples across the red, white and blue silk. The other items were stacked up against a bank. Owen had been giddy with excitement, leaping from one to the next like a starving man placed in front of a banquet table. In the end Jess had to insist on talking him through each in turn, but he had so many questions that after an hour they'd barely made it through a quarter of the atlas.

'So this country's called America.'

'The USA, that's right.'

'What's the USA?'

'The United States of America.'

'And the United States of America is in North America?'

'Right.'

'But this down here, this is America as well?'

'That's South America.'

'And this?'

'Central America.'

'And the whole thing together is . . . ?'

'America, yes.'

'So the country of America is in . . . America?'

'I think you're making it more difficult than it really is.'

Owen frowned and flipped to Southern Asia.

Jess rested her back against the rucksack and put her hand on the object wrapped up in her pocket. She closed her fingers into a fist to stop them trembling. Could she really do it? Could she really show it to him? The thing that not even her mother knew about.

'There's one more,' she said at last.

Owen's face lit up. 'Another present?'

'This one isn't to keep. And it's a bit strange, so you have to promise not to laugh.'

'Strange how?'

'It's . . . it's personal.'

He put the atlas to one side and sat down next to her. Jess took a breath and retrieved the item from her pocket. She carefully opened up the tissue paper, revealing a cone-shaped seashell. It had fractured into two pieces.

'What is it?' Owen asked, his eyes darting back to the

pile of books she'd brought him. 'It's broken.'

'I know that, Owen.'

He shrugged.

'My dad gave it to me.' Suddenly her mouth felt dry. 'We were on holiday when I was little. He went for a walk one morning and when he came back he had this for me. I remember . . . I remember it sitting on his palm. There were little bits of sand stuck to his skin. His hand felt really warm as I took it from him. I remember how warm it was. He told me that an animal used to live in this shell.'

'An animal? In there?'

'And then when the animal died the shell was washed up on the shore. It might have been there for a long time, he said, just waiting for someone to notice it and bring it to their lovely daughter as a present. His lovely daughter, that's what he called me. And then he kissed me on the forehead.'

Her stomach twisted itself into a knot and she fought to keep back the tears.

'I kept it on the table by my bed but after he left I knew Mum wouldn't want to see it, so I hid it in my drawer. Every now and then I get it out and look at it and I think about those little bits of sand on his fingers, and the way he kissed me on the forehead.'

'He's not around any more?'

'No.'

'Why?'

Because he realized I'd never be normal, thought Jess. And he didn't like that very much. Didn't like that at all.

She shook her head and pointed at the shell. 'It broke when we moved. I should have thrown it away, I suppose . . .' *Don't cry. You don't let them see you cry. Not ever.* 'Should probably have thrown it away.' *Don't, Jess. Don't.* But she couldn't help it. Tears splashed from her eyes and on to the frozen ground. 'Sorry. It's silly,' she said.

Owen reached out and rested his hand on hers. It felt like her veins flowed with freezing water. She looked up at him.

'I don't think it's silly at all,' he said. 'Not at all.'

She made her way along Weston Road and on to the High Street. She felt hollowed out and exhausted, and yet somehow stronger than before. Her arm still tingled slightly from Owen's touch – painful and comforting all at once. She was walking with her head bowed as always, and stepped straight into someone coming out of the chip shop.

'Excuse me,' she muttered, trying to make her way round. The woman placed a firm hand on Jess's shoulder. A rotten smell rose from her denim jacket. Jess shrank away in fear. 'Excuse me,' she said again, trying to keep the tremor out of her voice.

'Late, isn't it?'

'Can I go past, please?' Could she break her grip and

make a run for it? Every part of her wanted to get away, to get home, to be safe.

'Late for you to be out.' The woman's smile was unsteady. Thick fingers drummed a nervous beat on a shiny leather handbag.

'I know.' She jutted her chin out. *Don't let her see I'm scared.*

'How old are you?'

'Why?'

'Does your mum know where you are?'

'I'm twelve years old. What kind of a mother doesn't know where her twelve-year-old daughter is in the middle of the night?'

The woman's mouth opened, creating various additional chins below it. Jess continued to meet her gaze, turning on what her mother called the Stare. Jess had a wide forehead, narrow chin, and large, light grey eyes. She had long ago learnt that her natural expression of concentration produced an unwavering gaze that many adults found unsettling.

'You're cute,' said the woman eventually.

This was, Jess knew, a lie. She could be cute. She could, if she chose, be nothing less than adorable, but not unless she intended it, and certainly not when she switched on the Stare.

'Why don't I wait with you until your mum gets back?' the woman said. 'Where is she again?'

'I didn't say she was here, I just said she knew

where I was.'

The woman looked uncomfortable at this but was interrupted by a shout of greeting from someone across the road. Reluctantly, knowing it was probably wrong to leave a little girl alone in the street at night but with no clue what she should do about it, she took her hand away. 'Maybe you should just go home,' she said, turning.

'That's where I'm going now,' said Jess. 'You don't need to worry about me.' Relief coursed through her.

She started to move away but was stopped in her tracks by the sight of an extremely tall, thin man coming her way. He wore light blue scrubs, with an unzipped hoody over the top. It was Doctor Stannard, clearly on his way home from a shift. Her heart hammered upwards into her throat.

He was closing the ground between them quickly. A phone glowed in his hand, and for now he was intent on the screen, reading as he walked. It would only take a single movement of the head, though. Just one glance in her direction and the game would be up for good. All at once Jess could see her mother's face – skin drawn tight with worry, eyes red and sunken. There would be shouting at first, which would be bad. And then there would be disappointment, which would be worse. She would have to explain about her night-time walks, and any chance of slipping out again would be gone for ever. *Gone for ever.* She'd never see the ice garden again. She'd never see Owen.

The doctor was no more than ten metres away. There was no other option: Jess threw herself into an awkward hug against the woman's side, burying her face into the denim jacket. She could feel soft flesh squirming underneath. 'I just don't know where my mum is,' she said in a small voice.

'I thought you said . . .' the stranger began, but Jess began to sob quietly, her shoulders hiccuping with little jerks. She could feel the tension in the woman's body, but after a second a flat palm began to tap her back. 'There, there . . .'

She held on tight. From the corner of her eye she saw the doctor as he passed them. His high, bony cheeks looked stark in the cold light of his phone. Jess held her breath until the danger was past.

She waited a few more seconds and then abruptly took a step back. The woman shifted from one foot to the other.

'I'm fine now,' said Jess, 'thank you.'

'But your mum?'

Jess shrugged and offered a smile. Then, swiping a chip from the woman's paper bag, she broke into a run.

'I dare you.'

'I dared you first.'

'I double-dare you.'

'You can't do that.'

Friendly competition bubbled up between them like water from pressed moss.

'I bet you can't eat three ice-apples in a minute.'

'Give them here.'

'I bet you can't go down the slide forwards on your belly.'

'Just watch me.'

'I dare you to hang our flag from the top of that tree.'

'What if I slip?'

'If you don't do it, I win.'

'Then hand me the flag.'

'Vive la France!'

These bets were sealed with a solemn handshake, the winner gaining the right to set the next challenge.

'I dare you to cross the bridge to the forest,' said Owen, who was dangling from one of the arms of the Old Man.

Jess didn't look up, but her skin puckered and pimpled at the thought.

'Well?' he asked.

'Wait,' she said. She broke a piece of milk chocolate from the bar in her hand and held it out to the Flying Elephant Mouse, which was sheltering under a nearby shrub.

'You're stalling.' He leant down beside her.

'Stop it, you'll scare him off.'

'I'm telling you that's not the same one.'

'It is.'

'How do you know?'

'I recognize him.'

'They all look the same.'

'I recognize him, Owen. He's in training.'

'You can't be training him if it's a different one every time.'

'It's not. This is Arnold.'

'You called him Arnold? Why?'

'Because that's his name, of course.'

'The bridge, Jess. If you don't do it, then I win.'

'Come on little friend,' she cooed, 'just take a nibble.' She nudged the segment a fraction closer and the tiny creature's whiskers vibrated with interest. It inched forwards, eyes darting from Jess to the food and back again. Eventually it rose up on its hind legs and rested its forepaws on the chocolate. It dipped its head and took a tentative bite. 'Chocolate,' she whispered. 'I should have known.'

The mouse began to eat in earnest, its translucent face now streaked mud-brown. She reached down and carefully placed a single finger on the fur of its back. It kept eating. 'It's not running away,' she hissed, glancing up. Owen rolled his eyes. Jess began to stroke and the creature's body relaxed slightly, allowing her to trace the curve of its spine. *It's happening*, she thought. *At last!*

What followed was lightning fast. The mouse's eyes flicked up and Jess could have sworn they actually changed colour, from a brilliant blue to deep black. Its lips curled back and a throaty growl escaped. It leapt into the air, twisting to bring its mouth round to her finger. Jaws snapped and two rows of sharp, neat teeth sunk into flesh. She jerked away with a cry and the animal scuttled back to the safety of the flower bed. A few droplets of blood made blossoms in the snow.

'Did you see that?' said Jess.

'Let me have a look.' Owen made to take hold of her hand but Jess put a palm up to stop him.

'Too cold,' she explained.

He nodded and the two of them peered at the cut.

'You're red inside! That's disgusting.' Owen pronounced at last.

'Why would it do that?'

'It's a wild animal, what do you expect?'

'No, there was something else . . . I don't know. It changed. Its eyes.' The bleeding was already coming to a stop.

'So this is your excuse, then?'

'For what?'

'I dared you, remember?'

'Owen, I was bitten by a Flying Elephant Mouse! It might be poisonous.'

'Don't be ridiculous.'

'Have you been bitten by one?'

'I've never tried to pick one up.'

'I was just stroking it.'

'You're just trying to get out of it.'

Of course I am, she thought. The very thought of the bridge made her skin crawl. 'Bet me something else,' she said.

'Oh, come on,' he moaned, 'don't be so boring!'

'You do it, then, if you're so keen.'

'But I dared you first.'

Jess turned on the Stare but Owen met it with an equally powerful smirk.

She turned and stalked away. 'Well?' she called. 'Are you coming or not?'

*

The two of them stood side by side at the edge of the chasm – that dark, gaping mouth, twisted into an enormous grimace.

'Well?' said Owen.

Jess had a thick coil of wet rope inside her stomach. Bile washed up into her mouth. Her legs felt unsteady – the measureless darkness throwing her off balance. But a dare was a dare . . .

She stepped on to the bridge and heard the ice crack beneath. Every creak and groan made her wince. She didn't dare lean her weight on the handrail, which in any case stretched only half the distance across.

As she got closer the forest seemed to shudder. Leaves trembled on their branches in excitement at her approach.

'I don't know if I can,' she whispered.

'What did you say?' shouted Owen from behind her.

One foot in front of the other, Jess. Get to the other side, win the bet, and then run back as fast as you can.

But her feet wouldn't move. Her skin crawled as if thousands of insects were swarming over it. Her shoulders were locked and tight. 'I don't think I can,' she said, louder.

'So, you lose?'

'Think of another bet.'

'I'm actually happy with this one.'

'*Owen*.' Her voice was like a whip. Almost at once,

she heard him step on to the bridge behind her. He took her hand and again she felt that jolt of impossible cold. But now it was somehow comforting, as reassuring as a warm fire. She gripped his thin fingers and followed him back to the garden side of the bridge.

'You're shaking,' he told her.

She nodded her head, feeling sick. 'What's in there?' she said at last. 'What's in the forest?'

'I've never been in,' he replied, his eyes flicking up then quickly back to her, as if he couldn't even bear to look at it for long.

'Never at all?'

'No.'

'Not even to the edge?'

'The garden's my home.' He said it as if it were the most obvious thing in the world.

'You've never been curious?' she asked, not quite believing it.

As he shook his head a stronger gust of wind blew and the trees sung a brief lullaby in response. Swirls of powdered snow became dancers, moving around their feet and across the orchard floor.

'Then why dare me to go in?' asked Jess.

Owen looked down. 'I never really thought you would. It was just a bet. If you'd actually gone in there . . .' A shudder passed through his body.

'Owen?' she said. It was time to ask the question that had been running through her mind for days now.

'Who made the garden?'

'What do you mean?' he said, looking baffled.

'It's a *garden*. Someone must have *made* it. And if it wasn't you, then there must have been someone before.'

Owen shook his head.

'A mother or father?' she pressed.

'Nothing like that,' he said.

'There must have been!'

'There wasn't!' he snapped. The silence watched them. 'There wasn't,' he said more quietly.

'Owen,' she asked again, quietly, 'how long have you been here?'

'I'm not sure,' he said at last. 'I think maybe a very long time. Or maybe not long at all. Until you came, time wasn't all that important. All I know is I belong here.' He shrugged his shoulders in frustration. 'You think I'm strange, I know you do.'

Jess took a step closer to her friend and hesitantly ran her gloved fingers over his shining silver skin. Then, slowly, barely daring to breath, she drew back her sleeve to reveal the bandage on her arm. She loosened the tape around it and peeled it back to reveal the weeping wound underneath.

'You're hurt?' he said.

She took a deep breath. 'Have you . . . have you heard of vampires?' she asked.

'I don't think I have those here.'

'They're things that look like people but aren't.

Instead of food and water they live on blood. People are scared of them and think they're monsters.'

'Have you ever met one?'

'They're not real, Owen,' she scolded. 'But what makes them scary is that they only come out at night. People are frightened of anything that can only live in the dark. And that . . . that's me.'

'What do you mean?'

'I can't go outside in the sun. You see, where I come from, there's a sun in the sky. That's like a huge ball of fire and it burns me. My skin. It means I have to stay indoors or covered up all day so I always . . .' She swallowed a lump in her throat and went on, 'I'm always different . . . I always look different. Always *feel* different. I *am* different.' The words were pouring out of her now. 'I have a friend. Sort of a friend, I mean. He's in hospital and can't wake up. I read him one of my stories and so he feels like a friend but the truth is we've never even spoken. That's what it's like for me. My only friend might not even know I'm there. So there. That's it. I don't think you're strange at all, because I'm stranger than anyone.'

She waited for his response, chin raised in defiance while inside she broke into a thousand pieces. She waited for him to laugh or to tell her to go, but Owen merely dropped to his haunches and started scrabbling on the ground. Jess thought, not for the first time, that she didn't understand other people. Even frost-people it seemed. As she opened her mouth to speak he stood back up, holding out some kind of silver plant bulb. 'You haven't tried one of these,' he said, 'but they're really good. Better than the fruit even. Just don't eat too many at once.' He smiled at her and in that frozen place Jess felt warmer than she ever had in her life.

17

When Jess came through the hedge the next night Owen was sitting cross-legged on a boulder, drumming his fingers on the ice in a frantic, jagged rhythm. Arnold the Flying Elephant Mouse sniffed and scampered around on the ground by his feet. At the sight of her, Owen sprang up, sending the little creature scurrying away, and snatched something from the rock beside him. Before she could open her mouth to say hello, he'd jogged over and offered it to her, held lightly in his palm.

'I hope you like it,' he blurted out. 'I made it for you.'

Jess turned it over in her hands. It was a single purple ice crystal of a kind she hadn't noticed before. But, she was stunned to see, it was sculpted to resemble the seashell her father had given her that she'd showed him.

'Did I get it right?' he asked.

The shell was no larger than her thumb but Owen had carved it in intricate detail. 'How did you do this?' she gasped.

A scarlet wave rippled through the fissures of his body and the ice grass at his feet swayed back and forth. 'It just took time.'

It must have done, she thought. The ice itself was like nothing in Jess's own world: an impossibly rich purple, like the sky itself. The proportions of the shell were perfect, and the surface had been polished to a fine, flawless finish. She glanced up at him. He was shifting his weight from one foot to the other, clasping and unclasping his hands.

'Do you like it?' His eyes never left her, searching for reaction, his forehead ploughed with creases of concern.

'Are you joking?' she replied. 'Of course I like it! It's beautiful. Thank you!'

He gave a single, solid nod and was finally still. 'I'm glad,' he said. 'I thought it might help.'

'What do you mean?'

'You should take it home with you.'

'Wouldn't it be better off here?'

'Take it,' he said. 'I want you to.'

'But it would melt.'

'Jess, please.'

She searched his face for some clue as to why he was insisting, but he looked so earnest that she couldn't help but relent. 'I could . . . I could put it in the freezer, I suppose,' she said.

He nodded. 'That's what you should do.'

'Is there something you're not telling me?'

'No, nothing. I mean, maybe nothing. Just take it back with you. Please.'

Jess sprinted home, the world blurring around her like a painting in the rain. Her feet pounded the tarmac until she was dripping with sweat and could taste blood in her mouth. She came to a halt at her front door and sucked in a few draughts of air to try and calm her breathing.

She tiptoed into the kitchen and took the shell from her pocket. The surface was already beginning to melt; some of the intricate detail washing away and smoothing out to nothing. She wrapped it in a piece of foil and tucked it away in a corner of the freezer under a bag of peas that never seemed to get eaten.

That night she dreamt strange dreams – dreams that felt as real as her waking hours. She was standing in a frozen cavern. The ice was the same deep purple as the carved shell she held in her hand. She was afraid because she knew the sun was beating down on the top of the cave, melting it. She could see it getting thinner and thinner above her. Knife-like icicles scythed down, shattering on the ground all about. The sun did its terrible work, burning a hole in the roof until eventually a beam of light lanced into the chamber. There was nowhere to hide, no blinds she could draw. She was exposed. She braced herself for the burning pain she knew would come, but there was nothing. Nothing. Nothing to be afraid of. The sun was gentle and mild, and her skin welcomed its warmth. She stared around in wonder.

'I'm afraid Doctor Stannard's running behind time,' said the nurse.

Jess watched her mother's lips tighten in irritation. 'Do you know how long?' she asked.

'Only half an hour or so,' said the woman, wisely choosing that moment to vanish around the corner.

'*Only* half an hour,' said her mother. '*Only*, she says.'

'I told you we shouldn't have come.'

'We had to.'

'It's fine.'

'Doctor wanted to check you again.'

'We could have changed the bandage at home.'

'If you hadn't been so careless in the first place . . .'

'It was an accident. Haven't you ever had an accident?'

'Don't be cheeky, Jess.'

A man across the room glanced up at them. Jess and

her mother both fixed him with the Stare, not realizing the other was doing it.

'If we've got half an hour . . .' said Jess.

'Go on, then,' her mother replied, wafting a hand. 'Full Hat, though.'

Jess made her way to Davey's room and squeezed inside. It was much the same, like a time capsule preserving everything just as it is for the future. His chest rose and fell but his face, if anything, was even more washed out than before. Almost as pale as Jess herself.

She pulled off her gloves and took a pen and pad from her coat pocket. 'I'm so sorry, Davey,' she said. 'I haven't had time to write you another story. But I tell you what, I'll write you one now.' She began. *The Pod was the greatest of human inventions, for it could perfectly preserve a person for the two hundred years it took to travel to the human colony of New Earth.* She stopped, cocked her head to the side, crossed out the words 'New Earth' and replaced them with 'Avalon'.

'There's been no time to write anything new,' she explained. 'Wasn't meant to come until next week, but there's this thing on my wrist and they say it might turn nasty. Do you like stories about space? Not my usual thing. But maybe that's not bad. What if you're so stuck on what your "usual thing" is that you never find the thing you're really great at? Like, I wrote a story once about a girl living in the depths of the Amazon rainforest in a tribe that had never discovered the modern world. And this girl had it in her to be the greatest electric guitar player the planet had ever seen. Only, because of who she was, she'd never heard of either electricity *or* guitars, so that talent just stayed inside her and she never knew. It was a bit of a sad one, really. Do you like stories about space? I think I might try and write this one for you. I'll bring it next time if it turns out OK.'

Jess caught herself in the act of scratching at her bandage. Her mother and the doctors were right, of course. The nest of blisters was weeping and infected. It needed to be properly cleaned and re-dressed. Plus it was as itchy as anything. Or at least it *had been*. She realized that at that very moment the itching had stopped. In fact, there was no sensation at all. It felt normal. That was strange. She peeled away the bandage and peered underneath.

That can't be right, she thought. *That can't be right at all . . .* Her skin was perfectly smooth. The red, open sores that had been there just the night before had completely vanished, leaving nothing but a few dark freckles.

Impossible, thought Jess. *It was there. It hurt. It was hurting when I fell asleep. It can't just have vanished overnight . . .*

She stared and stared but there was no denying it. The burn, the wound, every last bit of damage had simply gone away.

Now that she thought of it, she felt somehow different all over. It wasn't a feeling so much as the absence of one – a lack of something that to her was normal and natural. It was her skin, she thought. Her skin felt different.

She remembered her dream. *That's impossible*, she told herself, but crossed to the window and put her hand on the blinds. Her heartbeat was loud in her ears. She took a deep breath, pushed her fingers through the metal slats and pressed them against the window. She could feel the warmth of the sun and braced herself for the awful, scorching feeling that would inevitably follow. But there was nothing. Her skin tingled slightly but other than that, nothing.

With a lump rising in her throat, she raised her hand to the string and pulled open the blinds.

'Remission?' said her mother.

'We can't say that,' replied Doctor Stannard.

'But that's what you call it, isn't it? When something like this gets better. What else could it be?'

'I'm afraid at this stage, we just don't know.'

'I didn't get burnt,' said Jess. 'I was standing right there in front of the window in Davey's room, right in the sun, and I didn't get burnt.'

'I realize that, but—'

'I always get burnt. With the thing on my arm I was

in the sun for, like, three minutes and you saw what happened.'

'Which is what we'd expect with a condition like yours.'

'So what just happened?'

'It's not possible,' said her mother. 'I asked. Don't you think I asked, time after time? We went to so many doctors in so many places and every single one said this isn't the kind of thing that . . . that she wouldn't get better. You said it yourself, Doctor. You told me that.'

She sounds upset, thought Jess, with a dawning sense of horror. *She sounds almost disappointed.*

'I haven't . . . that is to say, I don't know of any cases in which a condition like hers has spontaneously . . .' The doctor looked huge and lost. 'I'm not aware of any cases like this,' he repeated.

'Except,' said Jess, 'you are now. Aren't you?'

'We don't have the facilities here. We need to get you to a bigger unit, get other opinions, do more tests . . .' Now he was on firmer ground. 'Yes, that's it. We'll do more tests. We'll get the very best people on it, under my supervision of course, and we'll start ruling out causes. Don't worry, Jess, we'll get to the bottom of this.'

He's talking like it's a bad thing, she thought. *Like it's as bad as my condition itself.*

'How can this happen, Doctor?' asked her mother.

He ran fingers through his thinning hair. 'I . . . have no idea at all. We'll get you back in tomorrow and start to investigate then.'

'Will I stay this way?' Jess asked. *Please. Please let me stay this way.*

Please let me stay this way.

Please let this be real.

Owen was nowhere to be found. *Typical,* she thought. *The biggest news of my entire life and he's hidden himself away.* She trotted up the main path, shouting his name, but no response came.

She found him by the Old Man, staring up into its branches. 'I've been searching everywhere for you. Well, not everywhere, but quite a few places. Owen. Owen! Owen, I've got some news. Did you hear me? I've got something I have to tell you! Owen?'

A creeping dread spread through her.

'Owen?' she asked again, quietly, coming to his side, and when he finally looked at her she saw that his face was etched with pure despair.

18

One of her mother's favourite expressions was 'It's not the end of the world.' When Jess slipped and banged her head, for example, 'It's not the end of the world' was a comforting whisper in her ear. But when she sulked at being forced to do extra maths, 'It's not the end of the world' quite clearly meant, 'Stop being so difficult and do what I tell you.' Now, though, it was quite literally the end of the world and her mother knew nothing about it.

Owen raised his arm and pointed a single, trembling finger.

She didn't see it at first. She was about to ask what she was supposed to be looking at when all at once it hit her: there was a steady drip of water splashing from one of the high leaves.

She understood.

Water. Liquid water.

The tree was melting.

And if the tree was melting, then it was the end of the world.

If you weren't looking for it, you'd have thought nothing in the garden had changed. Flowers still glinted, the air was still sharp on the tip of Jess's tongue, and the grass still crunched under her feet. But now they were looking, Owen and Jess found signs of the melting all over. There was a trickle down the trunk of a fruit tree, a shallow puddle hidden deep in a flower bed, a sheen of moisture on the surface of a pebble. They even saw running water. It wasn't much, no more than a hand's breadth, but it snaked down the Sweep in a certain, continual stream.

The two of them watched for a long time, as if by doing so they could simply will it out of existence.

'What are we going to do?' Jess asked, at last.

'There's nothing we can do,' Owen replied, simply.

'So we just wait?'

'Maybe it will stop?'

'Or maybe it gets worse. Maybe the stream turns into a river. Maybe everything melts away. Every single thing. Even . . .' She stopped.

'Even me,' Owen offered.

'This is *impossible*.'

'No.'

'Owen—'

'It's not impossible, Jess. It's happening, isn't it? So it's not impossible.'

'Why are you being so calm?'

'How should I be?'

'There must be something we can do.'

'There isn't.' Owen dragged his hand through a hedge, sending up clouds of tiny ice crystals that swirled like motes of dust in a sunbeam.

'You can't just say that,' she said.

'Say what?'

'*There isn't*, and leave it at that.'

'Take my hand. See? Ice. I know what this means. I told you, the garden's my home. I know how serious it is. And there's still nothing we can do.'

'That's not good enough,' she snapped.

Owen shook his head. 'What would happen if you fell off a cliff?'

'What do you mean?' she said.

'I mean, if you slipped and fell, what would you do?'

Jess looked at him blankly.

'You'd do nothing,' he said. 'You'd just fall. And for those few seconds you'd know that it was all about to end but there wouldn't anything you *could* do. Flapping your arms, shouting, screaming – none of it would make any difference. That's what this is. It's just that

I'm falling slowly.'

She felt a surge of anger towards her friend. How could he not see how bad the situation was? 'We have to think,' she said.

'Jess . . .'

'Why's this happening? That's the question. Why now? What's changed? What started it?'

'Jess, just stop!' His face twisted in frustration and the snow whipped around his ankles.

'If we figure that out, then we might be able to stop it.'

'*Jess!*' Owen's brow creased and he clutched his temples, as if to grab some pain inside his head. 'There's no way. No point.'

'You're not giving up, Owen, I won't let you.'

'My head hurts.'

'The world's falling apart and you're complaining about a headache?!'

'Leave me alone!' he shouted. Jess took a step back, alarmed. Owen was shaking his head from side to side, moaning slightly under his breath. His blue eyes seemed almost grey now. 'No, no, no . . .' he slurred. 'Not this, not this.'

'Owen?'

He focused on her for second. 'Go,' he said, 'go and don't come back. Go! Please! Jess, please!' He doubled over in pain, his body trembling violently.

She took a few steps towards him and bent to look at

his face. It was as if dark clouds had gathered in the blue sky of his eyes. Without warning, he screamed. It was deafening – the howl of a mountain storm. All at once she was engulfed by a raging blizzard. Everything around her turned white and she had to grip a branch to stop herself being blown off her feet. A razor wind lashed her face. The noise was deafening and the cold unbearable, but worst of all she could feel the violence of Owen's anger, fear and grief swirling all around her.

And then it was gone. Her ears were ringing. Her face was crusted with frost. There was no sign of him, only a light set of footsteps in the snow marking where he'd turned and run.

'Owen!' she shouted, starting after him. 'Wait!' She heaved her rucksack on to her back and broke into a sprint, following his trail.

She hurtled up the path, pumping her arms and gasping for air, but knowing perfectly well she couldn't catch Owen in full flight. On she went, into the orchard. She caught her foot on a root and went sprawling to the ground. The eyes of a Flying Elephant Mouse peered out at her from under a leaf. She dragged herself up once more, emerged into the open and saw footprints heading over the bridge.

Not the forest, Owen, anywhere but there.

She couldn't stop, though. She couldn't leave her friend.

Jessica, no! It was her mother's voice in her head, but

she ignored it and hurried on to the bridge, barely breaking stride. The ice was slippery and the chasm yawned on either side. She felt as if she were balanced on the tongue of some vast beast and could almost hear the gurgling of its hungry belly below, could taste its cold breath around her.

With a blast of relief, she stepped off on to the far bank and, finally, paused. From the end of the bridge a narrow path cut directly into the forest. *A path.*

'Owen!' she shouted, and heard her voice echo through the trees, losing power with every repetition. The quiet was broken by occasional rustles in the undergrowth. *What's in the forest? What's waiting in there?* 'Owen!' she shouted again. How had this happened? How had the day on which the very thing she'd wanted her entire life – to be cured – finally come to pass, turned into this crawling nightmare? 'Owen!' she screamed, pouring every drop of power into the word until it turned into a sob that she had to choke back.

Nothing. Nothing at all.

She was startled by a loud beeping. Her watch. It sounded so artificial here. She shut it off and closed her eyes. It was time to go back. But how could she? How could she leave him in this awful place?

He'll calm down, she thought. *I'll come back tomorrow and he'll be in the garden and we'll work out what to do, how to fix this. And if not . . .* She couldn't finish the thought. If not would have to wait until tomorrow.

Jess reached her house and slipped inside. She hadn't gone more than two steps when she realized that something was very wrong. The lights were on. It was a few more seconds before she understood what that meant, and felt her heart drop from her body. She turned from the stairs towards the living room just as her mother appeared in the doorway. Her eyes were sunken and red, her skin as pale as paper and stretched tight. There was a stranger by her side. The stranger was a policewoman.

19

First there was relief, and a hug so tight Jess thought she might never escape it. She smelt the dying flowers of old shampoo on her mother's hair, felt the warmth of her body through dry skin.

Then came anger, its heat enough to scorch the walls.

'How dare you?'

Jess knew better than to respond.

'How dare you just sneak out like that?'

And in any case what would she say?

'I went in to check on you. Jess, are you listening to me? I said I went in to check on you! Do you know what that was like for me? Seeing you were gone and having no idea . . . no idea!' The shout clanged around the room. 'I thought you'd been taken. Do you hear me?'

Jess felt a new kind of sickness settle inside her. It wasn't a feeling she could remember ever having before. It couldn't be placed in a neat little box labelled with a word like 'guilt'. Guilt was when you took the last piece of cake when your mother wasn't looking. Guilt was something that came and went like a sudden gust of wind, whipping up debris behind it, for sure, but soon to be forgotten. This was different – deeper somehow. This was a wish that the things she'd done could be undone. That time could be rewritten so her mother never had to feel like this. So that her mother didn't have to look at her the way she was looking at her now.

She found a name for the feeling. *Regret.*

'I pray to God you never have to go through what I went through tonight, Jessica. That you never even have a taste of it. If anything happened to you . . .' Her mother pinched at the skin between her eyes. 'After everything I've done for you! And you just go walking off in the middle of the night where *anything* could have happened. Where anyone could have found you and . . .' She gave a sigh that was almost a moan, as if the last part of the sentence was too terrible to utter, as if she couldn't bear the ideas in her head.

What kind of a daughter would put their mother through that? Jess asked herself. *What kind of a person does that make me?* But even as she thought it, she knew that she would have to hurt her mother yet again. Because Owen was in danger, and his world was falling apart. She couldn't stay away and let that happen. She'd have to go back to the ice garden. Somehow she'd have to find a way.

The policewoman left them alone. They sat across the kitchen table, not speaking. There was no anger any more. A heavy blanket of sadness had fallen over the house and snuffed out those flames.

Say something, Jess thought. *Make it better.* But she realized that words alone couldn't help with that. Only time could.

Her mother made herself a cup of tea. One of the blinds had come away from its fixing and the washed-out glow of morning light began to creep through. Out of habit Jess got up and rearranged it. Only when it was done did she realize that perhaps she hadn't needed to. The thought sent her skin crawling. *Could it really be true?*

'Being out there, not wearing the Hat,' Jess began. *How to say it?* 'It feels different. It feels like . . . like something I need.' *Keep going. You owe her. She needs to understand at least some of it.* 'I don't do anything much,' she lied. 'I just wander around and think about what the places I see would be like in the day. There's a playground in Weston Park. I sit on the swings there.'

'As far as the park?'

'It's like I'm . . . like I'm getting out of my cage. Like I'm an animal who gets to escape for a few minutes.'

Tears welled in her mother's eyes. 'I never wanted you to feel that way.'

'It's not your fault.'

'I've tried, Jess. I've tried to make things be as good as they can for you.'

'I know.'

'I tried so hard.'

'It's not your fault.'

'How long? I mean, how many nights?'

'Just this last week.'

'And I had no idea.'

'Why would you?'

'I'm your mother. I should have known that something was different. I should have sensed it. Shouldn't I?'

'You didn't do anything wrong. It was me.'

'Why tonight, little one?' she said.

'What do you mean?'

'It might all be over. You might be . . .' Jess knew the end of the sentence. She might be *better*, so why risk sneaking out at all?

'You heard Doctor Stannard. Tests. More doctors. More people telling me what I can and can't do.' As she said it she realized it was true. She wanted to be cured but she dreaded what that meant. She was pleased she could be honest with her mother, even as she lied by not mentioning the ice garden.

'Don't you want to know what's happening to you?'

'Of course I do. But it's . . .' she tailed off.

'I understand, little one.'

There it was, unspoken. Jess was frightened of the tests that would begin that day. But her mother would make sure she went, just as the doctors had commanded. That was the right thing to do. The adult thing to do. You couldn't just accept a miracle and leave it at that.

'No point in sleeping now, I suppose. I'll make us some breakfast.'

'I'm sorry, Mum,' Jess blurted out. *And I'm sorry I'll have to leave you again*, she thought.

The hospital had insisted she still come in Full Hat. Until they knew what was really going on, it was better that Jess took no risks.

The needle stung as it punctured her arm, but she didn't look away. Instead she watched her very own blood flow up into vial after vial at the end of the syringe. There were more tests afterwards: things that scraped inside her mouth and lamps that shone on her skin.

'She's doing very well, Mummy,' said Doctor Stannard. 'Isn't she doing well?'

Her mother gave a thin smile. They hadn't spoken on the way there. There was too much to say and yet nothing at all.

Nurses came and went. The minutes swelled into hours. Another doctor was there, asking Jess all sorts of questions. He had a very deep voice, and bushy eyebrows that rolled away from his face like a pair of waves. Doctor Stannard sat in the corner of the room during this part, looking much smaller than usual. Jess started to write a story in her head about a giant who wakes up one day to discover he's become ordinary human size, which is all he's ever wanted. But instead of letting him enjoy it, the other humans keep him in a cage so that they can do tests and figure out what's happened to him.

Most of all, though, her thoughts went to Owen. Through all the talking and the poking and the prodding, she thought of her friend. Had he made it back to the garden or was he running still, deeper and deeper into the forest?

They handed her mother a piece of paper. Jess leant over to look. It was a timetable. The next few weeks of her life were laid out in a series of boxes and bullet points. *How can they expect me to do all that? How can they think that's OK?* This, then, was the price of wellness: not to be left alone until they'd taken all the joy of it away.

'Can I go outside?'

'Not for now, Jess. Not until we're sure there isn't still some damage happening that we just can't see.'

'Mum?'

'Listen to Doctor.'

'But—'

'I said listen to Doctor.'

'So, I'm better, but I can't enjoy it? I still need to hide away like some *thing*.'

Her mother's face flickered, as if she were flinching from a blow. 'Jess—' she began, but didn't get a chance to say more.

'I'm better. I'm cured,' Jess shouted. 'But I'm still not normal, am I? I'll never be normal to you.' She stood so quickly her chair fell backwards, clattering into the silence of the room. Without another word, she turned and left, but the moment she was in the corridor a wave of something unpleasant came over her. *You're making it worse*, she thought. Why was she snapping at her mother for something that wasn't her fault? But then why wouldn't she stand up to Doctor Stannard? Why wouldn't she take Jess's side just this once?

She realized she'd been staring into space only when there were shouts from behind her and she had to press herself against the wall to avoid being trampled by a pack of doctors and nurses who came hurtling along the corridor. She saw them all vanish through a door. All of a sudden, her blood went cold.

It was Davey's room.

She'd been so wrapped up in what was happening with Owen and in her argument with her mother, she'd barely thought of the sleeping boy. But now her fear for him came bubbling back up and she sprinted to the doorway.

There was a crowd of people clustered around his bed. Orders were shouted and actions carried out, but to Jess it seemed like nothing but awful, desperate chaos. Every now and then she caught a glimpse of him and was shocked to see how pale and broken he looked. The machine at his side was wailing a single, high-pitched note.

She eased into the room and stood in the corner, unnoticed. Her body felt as if it would turn itself inside out. Every sinew was drawn as tight as could be and her mind screamed, *Please let him be OK, please let him be OK.* All at once her head was flooded with the stories that she could write for him. Stories of genies being born from rocks amongst the desert sands. Stories of a child who could turn into a crow. Of a house that ate the people who came to live in it, of a girl who found a magical garden made entirely of ice. She would give everything, every ounce of soul, every drop of energy, every last spark of thought and kindness that she had inside her, if only he'd be all right. If only he'd be better. He had to be all right. He had to wake up. He had to hear the stories that she'd write for him.

Please let him be OK. Please let him be OK. Please let him be OK. Please let him be OK.

There was a hand on her shoulder. She jolted, as if woken from a nightmare. The room had emptied a little.

A smaller group of people milled around the bed but they moved without the frantic urgency of a few moments before.

Beep, beep, beep, went the machine.

'What are you doing here, Jess?' It was Davey's mother. 'Are you all right?'

'I saw them . . . I saw them all running in.'

'I know.'

'Is he? Is he all right?'

The woman trembled. She looked swamped by such sorrow that Jess could barely stand it. It was the same look she'd seen on her mother's face that very morning.

'Will he be all right?' she asked again.

'It happened yesterday for the first time. Days and days with nothing – no change at all. No better, no worse. And then yesterday, from nowhere, he started to crash. And now again today. The doctors don't know why it's happening all of a sudden. They say they're doing their best, but . . .' Davey's mother was silent for so long that Jess didn't think she'd continue. But eventually she spoke, in a voice that was barely a whisper. 'They say every time it happens it's less and less likely that they'll be able to save him.'

Everything went dim. Jess could hear a voice, her own voice, saying all the right things and promising to come back with another story, but it was as if it were all happening hundreds of miles away. Where she was at that moment there was only darkness and the rush and tumble of thoughts.

How had all this happened? Just a few days before, her life had been the most predictable thing in the world. She had her lessons, her stories, her mother, her trips to Doctor Stannard. And then it had caught light. Coming to see Davey, sneaking out at night, discovering the ice garden. But it was as if by opening the door to all that, she'd invited in complete madness.

Yesterday, she thought, *that's the key.* It was yesterday that her miraculous cure had happened. Yesterday that the ice garden had started to melt. Yesterday that Davey had crashed for the first time. Was it all a coincidence? Or was there something else going on, just behind? Something she couldn't quite see.

She came back to herself and discovered that she was in the corridor near Doctor Stannard's room. Sunlight streamed through the open window. It fell directly upon her face. She waited. Waited for it to burn her. But it didn't. It couldn't.

Jess closed her eyes and stood in the glow of the sun.

That night, her mother came into her room long after she would usually be asleep. Jess didn't open her eyes. Eventually she heard footsteps retreat. *Can I do this?* she asked herself. *Can I do this?* The question answered itself.

The wait felt painfully long, but at last she got up and pressed her ear to her mother's door. She heard breathing, slow and heavy, a sure sign of sleep.

Jess didn't bother slipping downstairs. She knew the door would be locked. Instead, she climbed out of the landing window and on to the flat roof of their kitchen. From there she scrambled down into the back garden. A passage led out to the street. The metal gate screeched as she pushed it open, making her wince.

She tried desperately to push away the mental image of her mother's tear-soaked face, but it remained stubbornly behind her eyes. And yet she had no choice – there would be time in the future to make it up to her, while this was her only hope of helping Owen. Of fixing whatever it was she'd done that had thrown both worlds into chaos.

The forest lay ahead and the forest was dark. The forest was a million different things all twisted around each other. It loomed, enormous, the trees and vines forming a dense, frozen mass. The forest was ahead of her and the forest was dangerous.

She'd searched the garden for Owen but had found nothing but more signs of the melting. He hadn't come back. There was only one thing she could do.

What's wrong with you, Jess? It was her mother's voice. *You left without any food or shelter, with nothing but a little bag over your shoulder. You have no idea where he is; you could be walking for days. You're meant to be seeing the specialists tomorrow.*

Jess's whole body trembled as she stepped out on to the bridge once more. The ice protested at every step, creaking and moaning beneath her feet. She knew she had to reach Owen, and yet her legs seemed disconnected from her brain – she had to will them to move her forward. Sweat gathered at her throat and on the back of her neck. She could hear the tremor in her own breath. 'Keep going,' she whispered, furious at herself for being so fearful. *You have to help him*, she scolded. *It's just a bridge and you have to help Owen.*

She was just over halfway when there came a sharp crack, as loud as a rifle shot. She stopped, frozen to the spot, heart thudding in her chest. She took another tentative step and felt the platform shift under her, the ice popping in warning. A fine crack appeared at her feet. She swallowed hard. The crack began to grow, snaking away from her, splitting off down new pathways as it went. She looked down for a moment into the hideous darkness and then ran. She drove with her knees, exploding into a sprint as the bridge gave way behind her. She pumped her legs as fast as she could and leapt the last metre, coming to land on the other side just as it collapsed entirely. She watched in open-mouthed horror as the bridge crumbled away into the abyss.

She pulled herself to her feet, swaying and stunned. She was alive, but she was trapped. She was trapped! There was no way back into the garden; no choice but to forge ahead. No choice but to go into the forest.

The trees around her were glistening, ragged teeth of ice. The trail twisted like an uncoiled rope up and down steep-sided ravines. As her eyes grew accustomed to the gloom, Jess could pick out birds and other small creatures. Eyes peeked out at her from the bushes. She could hear animals calling to one another. A Flying Elephant Mouse launched itself from a branch as she passed, and she gave a startled yelp.

She bent down and refilled her bottle from a trickle of water that wound its way through the undergrowth. The melting was spreading fast and there was no sign of Owen. No footprints or markers. Was he still running, never tiring, into the heart of the forest? How far might he have gone in the time she'd been away?

She couldn't tell how long she'd been walking for, only that her legs rang with a dull ache. There seemed no end in sight. Pinholes of sky peeked through the canopy. Jess trudged on, her feet completely numb from the cold. It occurred to her that if she were to die there, she'd never be found. No one would ever know what had happened to her. She shivered.

She came to a small clearing and sat down heavily, her legs giving out beneath her. She closed her eyes for a moment. *I could fall asleep here,* she thought. *I could rest.*

Something touched her.

Her eyes snapped open. A vine, hanging from one of the trees, had twisted itself around her arm. She shrugged it off, but another quickly took its place, cold and smooth.

Jess grabbed the creeper to free herself but it jerked hard, snaring her hand. She gave a cry of pain and snapped it off, leaving a bracelet of ice around her wrist. She pulled herself to her feet but tripped as another creeper slithered from the undergrowth. Her head cracked against the hard ground and Jess screamed – a very un-Jess thing to do. Screaming was for the kind of girl who lived her life in marshmallow pink. She didn't scream when the doctors put needles in her or when the sun ruined her skin. But she screamed now as more tentacles emerged all around her. They dropped down from the trees like snakes falling on their prey. They squirmed across the icy floor with astonishing speed, wrapping around every inch of her body and dragging her backwards into the deep forest.

A vine as thick as her wrist slid across Jess's throat, making her choke. The plant's grip was so tight she couldn't even struggle. Her chest was locked in a crushing embrace. Bright spots exploded in front of her eyes and there was a roaring in her ears like traffic thundering down a motorway. For a moment she was in a car at night, pylons rushing by, leaving trails of light in the black sky. She was in the front passenger seat, her mother driving, the two of them singing along loudly with the radio. Someone was shouting something, but Jess heard it as if through deep water. It seemed far away and unimportant. She was in the car with her mother and everything would be all right.

'Pull!' came the voice. 'Jess, help me pull!' A new sound penetrated the fog around her: the splintering and cracking of ice. She felt the vines loosen their grip very slightly and instinctively sucked half a mouthful of air into her lungs, opening her eyes as she did so. *Owen.* Owen was there.

Jess was amazed to find that she was still alive. She had a hazy memory of Owen flinging himself into the plants, tearing them off her body and dragging her free. Something tickled her cheek and she winced as her fingers found the cut just below her eye and prised out a shard of ice. The creepers were hovering around them, bobbing and twisting like serpents, waiting for another chance to strike. Exhausted, Owen pulled himself upright and took Jess's hand. 'Stay close to me,' he whispered as he took a step forward. The vines cringed, darting back a little but not retreating fully.

It's not him, thought Jess. *It's me they want.* She noticed that the plants were somehow fringed with darkness; it hung around them like a black halo.

'Jess,' hissed Owen, close to her ear, 'we need to *run*. Ready?' She gripped his hand more tightly and the two of them broke into a sprint, fleeing the clearing and returning to the path. They could hear the creepers desperately reaching out to stop their prey escaping. Jess and Owen didn't look back. They ran in single file, in the middle of the path, avoiding anything that might lash out from the undergrowth.

Jess was reminded of their first day together,

hurtling through the Maze. Owen had told her the garden unfolded. This forest seemed to do the same. She was suddenly convinced that if she was alone, she would be trapped there for ever. She could walk and walk and never find the end. But she wasn't alone, she had Owen. And this was his world.

As if answering her faith in him, she heard him bellow, 'There!'

She could see it: purple light breaking through the dense mass of trees. She ran hard, one final effort, and found herself stumbling into the open air.

21

'What are you doing here?' Owen asked. There was anger in his voice, but shy pleasure too. He offered his hand and Jess pulled herself up, brushing snow from her clothes with a gloved hand. Before them lay a wide, flat expanse, and beyond a vast range of ice mountains reared up into the sky.

'Don't *ever* run off like that again,' she said, jabbing Owen hard with her forefinger. 'Do you understand me?' And then she threw her arms around him, too relieved to care about the stinging cold.

'You're hurting me,' he managed.

'How did you find me?'

'I heard you shouting. I thought you might be in trouble. Why did you follow me?'

'I was worried, you idiot!'

'But I *hurt* you.'

'You didn't, see.'

'It happens sometimes when I'm upset. I didn't know how to stop it, so I ran away before I could make things worse.'

'I'm OK, Owen. Look. Look at me, I'm fine.'

The wind sang a sad song through the trees behind them.

'I'll take you back,' he announced.

'We can't.'

'What are you talking about? Of course you have to go back!'

She told him about the bridge, how it had crumbled away like icing sugar. Owen's face moved through a rainbow of emotions, from disbelief to horror, and it was all Jess could do not to throw her arms around him once more. 'We'll find a way back,' she insisted.

'There isn't one,' he replied, quickly. 'You've seen it. That bridge is the only way over.'

'I'll get you home, Owen. Don't worry. I will.' She heard her own voice, sounding strong and certain, and wished she felt so sure on the inside.

He laughed. 'Get *me* home?' he said, at last. 'What about you? What about me getting *you* home?'

In the forest she'd somehow forgotten, or wanted to forget, her own situation. She'd been so focused on the one goal of finding Owen that she'd pushed the bigger problem to the back of her mind. But of course, he was right – the white wall at the edge of the garden was the way back to her world. And if she couldn't get back to the garden . . . *Stop it, Jess. Stop that thinking right this minute.*

'What?' Owen asked, taking a nervous step back. For Jess had set her face and unleashed the Stare. 'Why are you looking at me like that?'

'You listen to me, right? I have a mother who's worried sick about me, so I'm going to find a way home. Which means *you're* going to find a way home as well. And on the way we're going to sort out this whole melting thing so that you've actually got a home to go to. Got it?' She turned the Stare up to maximum. 'I asked if you got that?'

He nodded.

'Right, then, there's no point us staying here. And if we can't go back, well, we'll just have to go forward. Maybe there's another way home. Another gap like the one in the wall.' *There has to be,* she thought, shivering. *Surely there has to be . . .*

The mountains grew ever larger. After some hours, the sky began to change. Thick, pregnant clouds rolled in and fat snowflakes, wider than saucers, drifted down. The snow fell heavier and heavier until Jess could barely see the path ahead and her clothes were encrusted with ice. The cold went right through her, slipping inside her bones, but she said nothing.

Instead, she thought of Mr Olmos sitting in his kitchen, sipping his evil tea. 'Jessica, let me give you some advice,' he would say. 'When they tell you that you cannot do something, you tell them they're all idiots and you just go ahead and do it anyway.' Grease-stained fingers would scratch that wiry beard. 'They told me I couldn't build a rocket in my garden. What did they know?'

'But you *couldn't* build a rocket. It didn't work.'

'That's not the point! I built something. I did it when they said I couldn't. *That's* the point.'

Owen had almost vanished from view. She stumbled to her knees in the deep snow, her heart like a bass drum in her chest. She cried out but the sound was lost in the wind. She shouted again, her voice tiny in the huge landscape. She was trapped in a swirling bubble of white. Shadows swam in the falling snow. *Give it back, girl,* they whispered. *Give it back.*

'What do you mean?' she shouted. 'Give what back? I don't know what you want me to do!'

A hand gripped her under the arm and lifted her. The shadows retreated and Owen's face took shape. He scooped her up in his arms and she listened to the banshee howl of the wind as her friend carried her onwards, with heavy, determined steps.

She thought of Davey, lying in his hospital bed with no one to read him stories. She wondered what his voice was like. It would be nice to hear it one day.

22

The path, which for so long had been dead straight, began to twist and turn upwards into the mountains. They rested a while for Owen to gather his strength. When Jess asked if he was all right, he simply smiled and said they should get going. Higher and higher they went, but the blizzard held visibility to almost nothing. Owen kept ahead and Jess followed, her legs burning with the effort of the climb.

Her mother had once bought her a Japanese puzzle box. It was a large, dark cube, the top and sides covered in intricate carvings. There was no lid, no hinge and no keyhole. Nothing at all that gave a clue as to how to open it. And yet, when Jess shook it, she could hear something moving inside.

Some people, grown-ups as well as children, would quickly have become bored and discarded the box. But Jess wasn't some people. After an hour or more, she noticed a small depression in the wood. It was almost invisible to the naked eye, but she was certain: a single leaf was fractionally out of line. She pressed the spot and heard a gentle click from inside. Now she was on to something. Patiently, she began to search with her fingers. Eventually she found two more switches. She pressed them, heard the catches release, and found that one panel could slide away. Inside there was another box, and another within that. On and on she'd gone, never discouraged, never for a moment considering giving up until finally she'd discovered at the centre a silver ring engraved with her name.

This journey was one enormous puzzle box, and Jess went on with the same determination. She couldn't begin to guess how much time had passed in her own world. Again, she pushed away the image of her mother's terrified face.

They took shelter in a shallow cave and shared some of the little food they had left. The ice-apple stung Jess's torn lips but it warmed her from the inside none the less. Owen lay down, curling into a ball. His eyes had turned a dull grey. There was no trace now of the colours that used to shimmer within him. It was clear to her that whatever was happening to his world had started to hurt her friend as well.

What are we doing? She thought. *We shouldn't be here.* If Owen hadn't run, if she hadn't followed, they would still be in the safety of the garden, plotting their next move. Yet the snowball had tumbled down the hillside, picking up size and speed as it went, and there was no turning back now.

'You never told me your news, you know,' murmured Owen at last.

'What do you mean?'

'When you found me by the Old Man. You said you had something to tell me.'

Jess couldn't help but laugh. 'I think I'm getting better,' she said, simply. 'I think my skin is becoming . . . I think *I'm* becoming normal.'

'That's good,' he said. 'That's extremely good.'

That's extremely good. She thought of the shell he'd carved of ice, tucked away in her freezer. Could it be? She wanted to know. Needed to. But she never would unless she could find a way back home.

'No one knows how it's happening. Owen?' She nudged him. 'I said no one knows how. Do . . . do you?'

But he'd already gone to sleep.

All at once a torrent of fear and desperation came rushing up through her and she clenched her fists so tightly that her nails cut into the flesh of her palms. She had to get home. She *had* to.

*

Jess woke with a start, thinking she was back in the hospital room, watching the doctors and nurses rush to help Davey.

As she sat up Owen rolled over in his sleep, murmuring. Her muscles complained as she eased herself off the hard ground and went to the mouth of the cave. The snow had stopped but the cold was every bit as savage. There was a roaring, rushing sound in the distance. She stepped outside.

This part of the path, she could now see, had been cut into the face of a towering cliff, and to her right the ground tumbled sharply away. It was a miracle that neither of them had gone over the edge in the blizzard. Her head swam. *One false step. That's all it would have taken.*

They were high up – far higher than she had realized. She looked out over endless miles of pristine white and could trace the line of the path back down the mountain until it ran straight as a railroad track across the snowy plain. She could see the gleaming forest and there, hazy in the distance, was a shimmering speck – the ice garden. All at once she was filled with a sense of hopelessness. She'd come so far in the hope of finding another way back to her world, but what if there wasn't one? What if there never had been? *What else could we have done, though?* she thought.

She followed the roaring sound, making her way along the foot of a scree-covered slope and into a narrow gorge. The path was barely wide enough for her to walk without turning sideways. She felt the most powerful sense of being watched, as if the world itself was peering at her with a fierce intensity. 'Hello?' she called, but of course there was no answer, just the rattle of her voice from wall to wall. *Hello, hello, hello . . .*

The roaring became louder. She sprinted up a steep slope, out of the gorge, and came to a halt, panting, where the cliff stopped and a view across the mountain range itself opened up. She couldn't help but gasp – there were waterfalls everywhere, thousands and thousands of them. They thundered and tumbled from every crystal peak – sparkling torrents falling hundreds of metres to the valley floor below. Clouds of vapour billowed and swayed. It was beautiful and awful. Here at last she could see the full scale of the melting that would eventually destroy the ice world, that would eventually destroy her friend.

And as she looked she had a feeling of utter certainty. All her frothing confusion was blown away. *I don't belong*, she thought. The ice world wasn't hers. She had been fooling herself that she could be part of it. She sucked in a lungful of air and sighed. The breath juddered from her body, turning instantly to steam. 'It's me,' she said. 'All of this. It's because of me.'

'No, Jess. Not because of you,' came a voice from behind her, and Owen was beside her on the ridge. 'It's my fault. I did it.'

*

'I hoped it would work,' he said. 'After that day when you told me about . . . about you. About your skin. I hoped it would work. Of course I couldn't know for sure. It was just an idea. And I definitely didn't know all this would happen . . .' he trailed off, looking out at the devastation around them. 'See there?' He gestured to a cliff face across the valley. Water poured from its lip and turned to smoke where the wind caught the spray.

Jess peered. There was a seam of deep purple running vertically from top to bottom, much darker than the ice around it.

'That's the bedrock,' said Owen. 'The ice that runs under everything. There are places where it juts out too, where it's right on the surface. It's like the . . .' He paused, searching. 'It's like the bones. Like the bones of those dinosaur skeletons you showed me in that book.'

She thought again of the shell he'd given her. It was the same purple, the same type of ice.

'Whatever my world is, whatever magic it has underneath the surface is locked away there in the bedrock. And after you left that night I started to think.'

'Owen,' she began, but he held up a hand.

'After you told me about your skin, I knew I had to do something to help. And then it hit me. The sky in this world doesn't harm you. But what if it's not about the sky at all? What if this world *itself* makes you better? And what if you could take it with you? So I took a piece of the bedrock, with all its power, and made you something. I didn't know if it would work . . .'

'It did.'

He smiled. Despite the ruin of his world, he smiled. 'I hoped it would help. But the moment you took it with you through the crack, it was like I'd been hit.'

'You should have called to me. Called me back.'

'It was like I'd been hit somewhere right in the middle of me. As if something had reached in and taken hold, a closed fist that was twisting and, and . . .' He dropped to his knees. His shoulders began to heave and he buried his face in his hands.

Jess stared. She wanted to drop to the ground and wrap her arms around him. But she found that she couldn't. She found that a sick-tasting kind of anger was welling up inside her and stopping her going to her friend. It grew and grew, a burning kind of fury.

'You knew,' she spat at last, surprising even herself with the venom of the words. Owen's head jerked up. 'You should have told me,' she said.

He looked as if she'd struck him. 'What do you mean?'

'You knew it was the shell. You knew why the garden was melting all along. There was me going on like an idiot about how we had to save it, but all the time you knew! That's why you wouldn't do anything. You could have stopped it, but you didn't want to!'

'That's not right. I wasn't sure, how could I be?'

'Did you know the melting would start when you gave it to me? When you gave me the shell?'

'Of course not! I didn't even know if it would make you better, I just *hoped*.'

Jess was barely listening. Her anger was hot and liquid. 'You should have told me. If you'd told me, I would have run home, then and there! I'd have brought it back and stopped all this!'

'Exactly!' Owen shouted back. 'I gave you something to make you better and if I'd told you what had happened, you'd just have thrown it away! You'd have thrown it away and let things go back to the way they were before! I didn't want that. I wanted you to be happy! I wanted you to be well!'

'But it's destroying your world!'

'That's up to me!'

'No, it's not!' she screamed. 'You're just like Doctor Stannard and my mother, thinking you can make all the choices for me! You should have told me! Why didn't you tell me? Why didn't you let *me* decide? It's my life!'

'How can you be so . . . so *ungrateful*?' he hissed. 'I was being your friend.'

'Friends don't lie to each other!'

'I did it for you!'

'Friends talk. Friends decide things together!'

'I didn't know the melting would happen! But when it did, you're right, I decided! I decided to let it happen. I let it happen for *you*!'

His anger rose to meet hers and with it came the storm. Jess was instantly engulfed by a raging blizzard, snow and ice tearing at her face. Or was it? Perhaps it was the claws of some unseen beast gouging at her flesh, or the needle-sharp teeth of a witch. Jess couldn't tell if she was standing or sitting, flying in the air or falling into a vast chasm. The physical pain she felt was swamped by a different kind of agony – a pure and terrible despair.

The ground began to shudder and shake. It was all she could do to stay on her feet. The mountain was bucking violently beneath her. Tiny fractures began to appear in the ice, quickly snaking and spreading.

There was a sharp crack and Jess jerked her head up just in time to see the slope above them give way. A raft of broken ice and heavy snow streamed down towards them. She tried to leap aside but her aching legs weren't quick enough. The avalanche hit hard. Darkness swamped her.

'Full Hat, Jess. Now, please.'

'Do I have to?'

'Why make it so difficult?'

'I'm writing a story.'

'Every single time, young lady.'

'I'm almost finished.'

'We'll be late for your appointment.'

'They can wait.'

'They will not wait. Why should they, just for us?'

'But my hair doesn't need cutting.'

'It's halfway down your back.'

'Mum . . .'

'Jessica.'

'They have to close the blinds for me.'

'They don't mind doing that.'

'There are always other people there.'

'And I'm sure they don't mind either.'

'It's embarrassing.'

'Jessica! Never let me hear that again, do you understand? You have nothing to be embarrassed about. Nothing in the world. You have *nothing* to be embarrassed about.'

Jess came to with a start, her mouth and nose filling with snow. She struggled to break free but there was too much of it, packed tight around her. She was buried. Hot tears pricked her eyes. How had she got it all so wrong? Her mother would never know where she'd gone. What would she think? That Jess had left her? That she'd run away and abandoned her?

There was a dull thud from above and then, after a moment, another. She closed her eyes to thousands of lights that shimmied and swayed in the darkness. Her chest burnt with the dying remnants of her last breath. It was like fire pouring through her lungs. She needed to hang on. If she could only hang on . . .

The thuds came more quickly now, as if someone were trying to punch through from the surface. *Owen*, she thought. She began to wriggle her body once more, using the last of her energy to help him in whatever way she could. The straightjacket of snow around her relaxed its vice-like grip and an air hole opened up near her mouth. She felt the breeze touch her nose and inhaled it greedily. The barrier began to shift and slide until, at last, a hand broke through and took hold of her. And then she was racing upwards, pushing herself along even as she was dragged, and in a moment she broke through to the surface.

With Owen's help she heaved herself free of the snowdrift. She was gasping for air and her forehead was sticky with blood. She tried to stand but one leg gave way and she cried out as she fell. Her ankle had ballooned up, puffy and tender to the touch. She lay on her back, breathing deeply, trying to wish the pain away. Flocks of ice-birds formed V-shapes in the clear sky above.

She stood again, more gingerly this time, testing how much weight her leg could bear. It was unbelievable. The mountainside was in ruins. Where before there had been pristine snow, there was now a mangled wreck, the surface scraped away to reveal hard, grey ice below.

Owen stood a little way from her, his shoulders hunched, eyes turned away. She could sense the shame flowing off him in waves.

'It's not your fault,' she said in a bruised voice. 'Are you listening to me?'

'I can't control it.' She realized that he was shaking, trying with every last bit of himself to stop the storm from rising up once more. Flurries of snow whipped around him.

'Owen?' she said. 'Owen, it's all right. I know you didn't mean that to happen. You saved me.'

He looked up at her and she couldn't help but stumble backwards, her ankle screaming. His eyes had turned black. But not just black, a black beyond black, which she recognized. She had seen it before, when the darkness in the Maze had reached out to swallow her. She had seen it the moment before the Flying Elephant Mouse had sunk its teeth into her hand. She had seen it hovering around the vines in the forest.

'It wants to hurt you, Jess,' he said. Every word seemed an effort.

'What does? What wants to hurt me?' But she knew. The blackness in his eyes was the dark heart of the ice world reaching out to destroy the intruder.

'This place,' he said. 'My place. It doesn't want you here.'

She flinched away. 'But why?' she asked. 'Why can't I be here?'

A look of pain passed over his face and he shook his head. 'I do though, Jess. I want you here. But I don't know if I can control it.'

She went to him. He jerked back, but she put her arm around his shoulders and squeezed. The searing cold was still there but didn't burn her like it had before. There was something stronger than that between them now. The darkness in his eyes clouded a fraction, as if he was mastering the destructive power welling up from inside. He was her friend. He was the best friend she'd ever had, and there was no way in the world she was going to leave him when he needed her the most. When he couldn't even trust himself.

'We have to keep going,' she said. 'There's nothing else we can do.' She took his hand and together they started forward over the wrecked slopes to wherever the path might lead.

It was a cave. A dark mouth that gaped at them from the mountainside into which the path disappeared. With what felt like the final morsels of her strength, Jess struggled up the slope and stepped into shadow.

They hurried on as best they could, leaning on one another for support. They followed the path, just as they had for so long. The cave became a tunnel that twisted and curved like the body of a python. It was lit by glowing jewels that studded the walls and floor. Eventually they emerged into an enormous chamber at the heart of the mountain. The ceiling was so high it could barely be seen. This was the end of the path. The end of their journey. The only place they could have gone.

And it was empty. There was nothing. No gap back to her own world, no clue how to help Owen. Jess realized she'd been clinging to a fragile ball of hope that now crumbled and flaked away in her hands. She gaped, trying to make sense of it all.

Owen staggered to the centre of the chamber. His eyes had lost that terrible searching darkness, and were now a smoky grey. His head fell forward and he dropped to his knees.

'Owen!' she shouted in alarm, running to his side.

'I'm sorry,' he said, and it seemed to Jess that he spoke with two voices at once. One was that of the boy she knew so well while the other sounded older than the mountains themselves. He looked up. 'I'm so sorry that I hurt you.'

'No, it was my fault. You were only trying to help me. I should never have shouted at you. You were right, I was being ungrateful. All the time you were only trying to help me.'

He was crying, she realized with a jolt. A tear formed in each eye, swelling and growing until they spilt down his cheeks where they froze once more. All of her pain faded away as she realized what it meant. *The melting's started inside him.*

'I shouldn't have got angry with you. I get so frustrated. No one ever lets me decide for myself. That's all. I'm sorry, Owen. I'm so sorry.' Her own tears joined his.

'The things that attacked you in the forest, Jess,

they're not *thinking*, not like you and I think. They're reacting, working on instinct.' He tailed off for a moment. 'They want to punish you, even though it's not your fault.'

I'm like a virus in a body, Jess thought, *and the body is fighting back*. 'And you?' she asked.

'It's all connected. This whole world is connected and I'm part of it, just the same as a flower growing in the garden or the highest mountain peak. I'm *me*, I'm Owen. But I'm also *all of this* and there's a bit of me deep in the middle that works on instinct too, and I can't control that. That's where the storm comes from. That's what hurt you.'

'I don't belong here,' Jess murmered, and Owen hung his head.

'I thought . . .' she began, but found the words wouldn't come.

'You thought the garden was for you,' he finished for her.

Anger flared once more, sudden and hot. 'If I wasn't meant to be here, then why did this stupid world even open the door to me in the first place? No one else found it, just me! Why did it let me in?'

At last Owen spoke. 'I don't remember a time when I wasn't on my own. And I was happy because I didn't know anything else . . . But then one day I thought I heard a voice.'

Jess frowned. 'What do you mean?'

'It was faint, but if I stood very still I could make out whispers swirling in the air. And after a while they started to make sense. They were stories. Stories about things I didn't understand, about places I'd never seen. Some were just ideas and others created whole worlds.'

Jess felt her breath run short with the impossibility of it all. 'And then one day the voice sounded stronger. Closer. More *real*. I put my ear to the ice wall . . .'

'Go on . . .' She couldn't help but shiver as the pieces started to come together in her mind.

'It seemed like it was just there, just on the other side. It was talking about a place full of children. About two girls climbing together and their mothers sitting and watching.'

A hard lump began to form in Jess's throat.

'I had to see. To know. I was afraid, but the thought grew and grew until there was nothing I could do but act on it. I touched the wall and it was as if I could feel every molecule. It looked so solid and yet I saw how thin it really was, this edge of my world. I pulled my hands apart and a crack began to open. I pulled and pulled until I'd made a gap wide enough to slip through.

'It was so dark. The air tasted wrong and the heat was awful beyond belief. But I didn't care, you see. Because I could hear the voice more clearly than ever. I knew that it was close by.'

Jess thought back to the night she'd found the

garden. She remembered sitting on the swing, describing the imaginary children around her, and all of a sudden shivering, as if struck by an icy blast of air.

'It was so hot. I knew I couldn't go any further into that world but I didn't want the voice to fade away again. So I left the door open a crack and hoped it would find me. And it did. It came one evening and told me a story about someone called a tailor who made everyone angry and who had to run away. And I was happy. But then I saw you in the woods and realized what I'd done. I'd let a stranger into my garden.'

'That's why you were so angry.'

'Not angry. Afraid.'

'I get those two confused as well.'

'And then I gave you the shell and started all this.'

'You should have told me what it had done. When you realized. As soon as you realized.'

'And take back that gift?'

'Yes.'

'It makes you better, Jess, that's what matters. If you destroy it, you'll go back to how you were.'

An image of the playground leapt into her mind. Not shrouded in darkness but bathed in egg-yolk sunlight. And her, in the centre, swinging back and forth.

She clenched her jaw. 'You're being ridiculous,' she made herself say. 'You've seen the waterfalls. The damage. Before long this whole world . . . *you*. I can't let that happen. Not even for . . .' *Bare arms. Lying in the grass. A sandy-haired girl calling me to play football.* 'Not even for that.'

Her body swam with sickness.

'But that's it,' said Owen, 'that's the choice. There's no other way.'

There's no other way. In taking the shell home with her, she'd fractured this world and all the power was leaking out. It was like puncturing a plastic bucket and watching the water squirt and spray on to the grass. She could save the ice garden by letting the shell melt away, but in the process her cure would vanish. Or she could keep it, and live a life like everyone else. She could go outside. She could make new friends. But Owen and his world would fade for ever.

She thought of the two of them, chatting under the branches of the Old Man and throwing themselves down the slide. Hiding in the Maze. She couldn't let it happen, of course she couldn't. She couldn't be so selfish.

She heard children shouting on their way to the park. Children she'd never get to know. Closed curtains and stories in a book. Telling tales to a boy who might never wake up.

Grief came as if dragged out of her. She cried tears of frost. 'I can't,' she managed to get out, at last. 'Owen, I can't let you die.'

'Jess,' he said quietly, shaking his head. 'I won't let you throw it away. You have to promise me. You *have* to . . .' he tailed off, exhausted by the effort of talking, and all at once tumbled to the floor.

'No!' she shouted, falling to her hands and knees beside him. His skin was damp and his breath came in ragged gasps. 'No,' she moaned. *You can't die. Not because of me. Please, not because of me.* It seemed to her that for a moment she heard a high, flat beep, like the one from the machine in Davey's hospital room, but it might only have been the wind gusting through the tunnels.

'You have to go, Jess. *Go.*'

She began to protest, but he raised one trembling finger and to her horror she saw that the walls of the cave were beginning to warp as they melted. She looked around, wide-eyed, unable to fight back a sense of wild and uncontrollable panic.

'Go,' he said again, groaning with the effort of speaking.

'It doesn't matter, Owen. Even if I promised you. There's no way back. I'm trapped here just like you!'

'No, you're not. Look.'

And then she saw. On the far side of the chamber, where the trail ended, was a smooth white wall slightly different to all the others. Exactly like, in fact, the one all the way back in the garden. She couldn't believe it. She'd told Owen they needed to keep moving, but only because there had been no other option. But the path had brought them to another way home after all.

'I can't leave you,' she said, but knew that she had no choice. If she was to help her friend, she had to go back to her own world. She had to destroy the shell. *I'm going to save you, Owen,* she thought. *I'm going to save you.*

She planted a kiss on his forehead and dashed to the wall. Water was pouring down it now and, when she placed her palm on the ice underneath, it felt as fragile as an eggshell.

She struck it. The surface fractured. Again and again she struck until she'd made a crack large enough to go through. She turned back to Owen, who had pulled himself up on to one arm.

'You're not strange, Jess,' he managed to get out. 'I know you think you are, but you're not. You're different. And that's good. That's *perfect*.'

'I'll never see you again.' Her voice cracked. 'You're my only friend.'

'Don't forget me,' he said.

'Don't be ridiculous,' she replied.

'Promise me. Promise me you'll keep the shell. Promise me you'll *live*.'

She stepped backwards through the gap, under the freezing waterfall.

His face disappeared from view.

25

Jess was warm – a strange feeling after so long. She took a breath, tasting the dusty-sweet air. There was no ice, no cold, no raw wind whipping across her face. Everything was still and everything was peaceful. There was rest. There was warmth.

She was snow-blind, unable to see, and it took a few moments for the colours to form into solid shapes. One blur in front of her became a set of swings, another a climbing frame. All at once, as if a switch had been flicked, sounds rushed in: the shouts of children and the dull burble of adult conversation.

'Of course the real problem's with the teachers!' a scarecrow-like woman said to an extremely large man. 'You'll get nowhere *telling* Jacob what to do, you have to *ask* him.' The man wheezed and coughed in agreement.

It couldn't be possible. It beggared belief. All those miles, all those thousands of steps and yet here she was, curled up on the ground at the entrance to the play-ground. *That's not the important thing,* she thought, dimly. There was something else, something she was missing. Her thoughts were moving too slowly, like honey dripping from a spoon. She had to think. She had to remember. *Think.*

'Gosh, are you OK?' The scarecrow was coming towards her, while the man stood behind, cow-like. 'I didn't see you lying there. Is everything all right? How long have you—' The woman broke off mid-sentence, the rational part of her mind rejecting the suggestion that this girl had somehow appeared from nowhere.

'Think,' said Jess.

'I'm sorry?' replied the woman.

'Think,' she said again. And then it all came rushing back. The chamber at the heart of the mountain. The walls melting. Owen crumpled and in pain. *The shell.* She had to destroy the shell.

She leapt to her feet but immediately cried out as pain knifed through her injured ankle. The woman took a step back in alarm and Jess understood how strange she must look in her soaked and filthy winter clothes, streaks of blood across her face.

What was she to do? She felt herself spinning on the spot, desperately seeking . . . something. *Get yourself home. You need to destroy it. No matter what you said to him. Get yourself home now . . .* Home. Her mother. The ball of guilt she'd managed to keep down inside surged up her gullet, and she felt sick to her stomach. She had to go home. *But how can I? How can I face her?*

She dragged her injured foot behind her and grabbed on to the railings as she made her way up to the road. The sounds and smells were baffling. The cars were too many and too quick. She could see the exhaust trailing from them, vanishing into the soupy summer air. Almost everything was grey and what colour there was – the painted and the plastic – was artificial and gaudy. She turned up the hill towards the centre of town.

It must have been a Saturday, because the streets were packed with shoppers. This was a scene Jess had only ever seen from behind the tinted windows of her mother's car. She had always yearned to be in the midst of it. But now the people were in her way and she was forced to dodge and weave through gaps as best she could with her damaged leg. She caught her reflection in a shop window – a tiny figure wrapped from head to toe in thick clothing. People stared and whispered to one another. Seconds later, though, a familiar voice rang out and a hand clamped around her shoulder.

'Jessica?' the voice said. 'What are you doing here? My word, what's happened to you?'

It was Mr Olmos from number thirty-three. 'Please,'

she said, 'take me home. I need to get home now!' And with that she collapsed into his arms.

Mr Olmos carried her through the sliding doors and into the lobby. 'I need someone!' he shouted. 'I need a doctor!' but to Jess his voice sounded far away. Her head was swimming, the world becoming blurry and faded. Only her pain seemed real, like a burning ball in her mind.

She was lowered into a wheelchair. There were people all around. She could hear her neighbour asking loudly if she'd be OK, and a soft voice murmuring to him in return. She tried to speak, to explain that this wasn't right, that she needed to get home, but her throat was too dry.

She saw a flash of white coat at her elbow and a tall figure bent down beside her. 'My God,' said Doctor Stannard. 'Jess . . . Look at me, Jess. Where have you been? The police came here. Asked questions. Where have you been? Thank God. Thank God you're safe.'

Another wash of dizziness came and went. Her head was too heavy, muscles like the embers of a dying fire. Doctor Stannard and his colleagues spun around her wheelchair like figures on a carousel. Their voices became more and more remote. She closed her eyes and fell into the darkness.

26

There was someone nearby, silhouetted by a light from behind. *Owen?* No, it couldn't be. Not a child at all, in fact. Taller. Very tall. The figure moved. He was peering down at a chart, with a familiar half-frown on his face. *Doctor Stannard.* Jess watched through half-closed eyes, not wanting him to know she was awake. That conversation could wait. She sat up only when he'd completed whatever it was he was doing and vanished behind the curtain that was pulled around her bed. Her body was a rhapsody of pain, but that wasn't her main concern. She had been asleep. Asleep! And with every minute she wasted, Owen was in greater danger.

Fragments of conversation floated down the ward.

She saw her mother's coat lying crumpled over a chair. Jess could have sobbed at what she had to do, but this time at least it would only be for a few hours. She'd sneak out of the hospital, go home, and destroy the shell. Owen and his world would be safe. And then her mother could shout and scold her all she liked, and Jess would take it without complaining, because what she'd done had been awful. The right thing, but awful all the same.

She slipped her legs out of bed and pulled on her shoes, trying one last time to block out the pain. But before she could get any further, she saw the curtain twitch and a head appeared.

It was her mother.

They stood, frozen, for a moment, each shocked at the condition of the other. Jess braced herself for the oncoming storm but instead found herself wrapped in an embrace she hoped might never end. Her mother's perfume was in her nose, sweeter than any flowers, richer than baking bread. Their tears were damp on each other's faces. At last they separated and, instead of shouting, her mother bowed her head and said, simply, 'I understand.'

Jess didn't reply. What could she say? How could she explain?

'When Doctor started talking about all those tests you'd have to go through, going to London, to specialists,

I understand – you got scared. Thought you couldn't face it. And then we argued and that was the final straw so . . . so you went. You just went.' Her voice was choked to almost nothing. 'My god, I thought I'd lost you . . .'

'I'm sorry,' Jess said at last. 'I'm sorry, Mummy.' She never used that word, not any more, but it came easily now. 'Can we go home?'

'We will. Soon. I just need to fetch Doctor.' Jess shook her head but her mother went on, 'He'll want to see you, to look you over.'

'He was just here.'

'Now that you're awake, I mean.'

'No.'

'They say your ribs might be broken, and your ankle looks awful, and . . .'

'I just want to go home.'

'You have to let Doctor look at you.'

'I need to go home, Mum.' What if they kept her there? What would happen to Owen then? 'I need to go home now.'

'No, you need to lie back down in that bed until they can be sure there's no major damage. And then you need to tell me where on earth you've been!'

'Will you just listen to me?'

'Get back into bed, Jessica.'

'No.'

'Don't argue with me.'

'Mum, please.'

'Doctor says you'll have to stay overnight at least.'

Overnight? She thought of the waterfalls thundering in the ice mountains, the impossible tears welling in Owen's eyes. Too much time had gone by already. Her mother was still talking but the words made no sense. Eventually Jess could take no more of it and cried out, 'I know what's best for me!'

Her mother stopped, a look of shock on her face.

'I know best, Mum. I know what's best for me and I know what I have to do. You always listen to Doctor Stannard! Always do what he tells you to, even when I say it's not something I want.'

'I know it feels like you're very grown up, Jess, but you're not, not really, and sometimes you have to listen to what adults tell you. I'm your mother, he's your doctor, and you're only twelve years old.'

'And I know what's best for me. Not always, maybe – fine, but some of the time at least, and right now I'm telling you that you *have* to take me home. Please, Mum. Please. I'll explain everything, I promise, but for now you just have to trust me.'

The curtain screeched as it was swept open by Doctor Stannard. 'I thought I heard voices. She's awake, Mummy, that's good news.'

Jess didn't take her eyes off her mother. Her face was criss-crossed with lines and there were dark circles above her cheeks. *Please,* she thought. *Just this once, trust me. Please.*

'I'm sorry,' her mother said at last. Jess's heart sank, but then she saw her turn to the doctor. 'My daughter needs to be at home right now.'

It was strange, stepping through the front door of her house. It turned out she'd been away for two days, but she felt it was a different girl who came home that afternoon.

Doctor Stannard hadn't been angry so much as baffled. He wasn't used to being ignored and Jess had taken sly pleasure in his stuttering protests.

'Well, we're here,' said her mother. 'Will you tell me where you've been?'

'Soon,' said Jess, as she made her way into the kitchen. She opened the freezer drawer and rummaged around until her fingers closed on the small, foil-wrapped parcel.

Then she hurried out into their postage-stamp back garden. *How will I know?* she thought. *What if it's already too late?* But when she unwrapped the shell and held it in her hand she felt something like a pulse – the beat of life – coming from it and she was certain: Owen was still alive. She could save him. Save it all.

Her mother watched her from the door and Jess wondered what was in her mind at that moment. Was she only thinking of the last few days? Or was she marvelling at the sight of her daughter standing in the full glare of the early afternoon sunshine?

She began to cry. She couldn't help it. The sun was so soft and so warm; soothing and nourishing all at once. *I could have had this*, she thought. *I could have had this for the rest of my life.* But she couldn't, of course. Not at the price it demanded.

She balanced the shell on the palm of her hand and watched as it slowly turned to liquid, enjoying every last ray of light lapping her skin and fighting the sense of loss that threatened to send her to her knees. She pictured Owen's face and that gave her the courage she needed. This was the right thing. And she had this moment – one final, brief moment under the sun.

At last there was nothing left but a few droplets of water, which she let run through her fingers and on to the grass. She turned to her mother, barely able to see for the tears. She could feel her skin starting to tingle as the gentle sun became once again what it had always been for her – an enemy.

'I need to go inside now,' she said. 'And we should draw the curtains.'

27

The idea of the hospital filled Jess with horror, but she knew she had to go back. Her ankle had turned a sickly yellow and her ribs groaned. But none of that mattered to Doctor Stannard as much as the sudden return of her condition. Why had it gone and why had it come back? He faced both questions with the same clueless bafflement. He brought in colleagues and she was tested, poked and prodded until finally her mother pronounced that she'd had just about enough of it all and, if they didn't mind, she'd be taking her daughter home again.

Through it all Jess barely listened. After all, she knew exactly what had happened to her. And besides, she had something more important to do. She had to visit Davey.

Her mother came with her, holding her hand as she limped through the hallways. As they got closer and closer to his room Jess felt her chest tighten. All she could think of was how he'd been on her last visit. She wanted to turn back. She wanted not to know, feeling she couldn't face the bad news. She'd saved Owen but had lost him in the process and had lost her own cure too. To lose Davey as well would be almost too much to bear, she felt. And yet there was a nagging voice at the back of her mind. Owen had said he'd heard her reading stories, but how could that be? There was only one person she'd read them to.

Soon they were outside the door and her mother nodded for her to go in. The handle was cool to the touch. She took a final breath.

She pushed.

She stepped inside.

And she grinned.

Davey was sitting up in bed, leaning back against a couple of pillows. He was thin – in need of a few good meals. But he was awake. Awake and reading from a slim stack of papers in his hand.

'You're all right! You're better!' she cried, and immediately turned bright red. 'I mean . . . hello.' She waved, and felt stupid for doing it. *Say something else*, she told herself. 'Nice to see you up,' she managed, and waved again.

Mousy hair tumbled over the boy's forehead. His eyes were a deep and brilliant blue. Jess realized she'd never seen them before. 'Hello,' he said in an accent she couldn't place. 'Are you lost?'

Jess opened her mouth to speak but thought better of it. What could she say? *Well, this might seem a bit strange, but while you were asleep I kind of started visiting you, so even though you don't know me at all, we're actually friends now, I hope that's all right with you*. 'No, I'm not lost,' she mumbled. 'I just came to see how you were.'

The boy frowned, as if considering something. Then he nodded. 'You're Jess, aren't you?' He held up the papers in his hand. 'You're the one who brought me this story.'

She turned a deeper shade of crimson and her heart tapped out a skittering beat. 'How did you know it was me?'

'Your voice. I recognized your voice.'

'I knew you could hear me! I told my mum you could, and Doctor Stannard too.'

'Of course I could hear. Well, no, that's not right. It wasn't like I'm hearing you now. I don't mean that. Don't know how to explain it really. Sounds mad. But I could hear them, your stories. Almost like dreams. Like I was dreaming them. Like I was living *in them*. And then when I woke up I found this by my bed.'

'You got better,' she said, shaking her head. 'You

really got better . . . The doctors told your mum you might not.'

'They don't know what's going on, I don't think. Keep coming in here to look at me and then vanish off to have a little chat. I don't think they know what they're talking about.'

'Tell me about it!'

'Right. But the thing is, they thought I was getting worse and worse. And then all of a sudden, a few hours ago, I just opened my eyes. I'm a medical marvel, apparently.' He smiled, proudly.

So was I, Jess thought. *Briefly at least.* Then she was struck by something else. 'A few hours ago?' she asked.

'That's right.'

A few hours. It had been a few hours since she'd stood in her garden and watched the shell melt away.

'Hey, do you live here? In town, I mean,' asked Davey.

'Yes.'

'We moved here. Like, a week before my accident.'

'That's bad luck.'

'You're telling me. Can't make new friends when you're asleep, can you?'

'I'm sure you'll meet people.'

'At school, I suppose. Maybe we go to the same one?'

'No. I don't . . . I get taught at home.' Again, she felt a stab. She could have gone to school, but now she never would.

'At home? That's cool.'

'Is it?'

'Course it is. Gives you, what do you call it? Mystery.'

'Does it?'

'Course it does. Makes you different. Who wants to be like everybody else, eh?'

Jess glowed.

'Did you finish the space story, by the way? Sounded like a good one.'

'I didn't get a chance.'

'Well, whenever it's ready.'

'Yes, sir.'

Davey grinned at her. 'And what about the other one?'

'What other one?'

'The other one you told me.'

Jess shook her head. 'I don't know what you mean. There was just "The Unfortunate Tailor".'

'No, you know – the really mad one. I mean, this one's mad but *that* one was totally crazy.'

Jess felt her head start to swim. 'What was it about?' she asked.

'I don't remember it all. Like I say, it was all pretty strange. But it was about some kind of garden.'

28

Her cure might have gone, but it left a trace. She wasn't able to go out in the sun but, if the clouds hung thick and low and she lathered herself in the strongest sun cream, she could walk uncovered to the shop at the end of the road and back. Some part of the garden's power had stayed with her, she supposed, and she was grateful.

The next Sunday Jess and her mother made roast lamb with Yorkshire puddings. Afterwards they shared the washing-up and drying.

'It wasn't because of you,' Jess offered, at last.

Her mother stopped, a serving bowl held out in front of her. She lowered it slowly on to the sideboard. And then, in a gesture that was completely unlike her, she knelt down.

'It wasn't because of you,' Jess said again.

'Will you tell me where you went?'

'You wouldn't believe me.'

'Try me.'

'One day.'

'Will you at least promise me you'll never do that again?'

'Never.'

'Never ever?'

'Never ever.' Jess nodded and for the first time in days a smile broke across her mother's face.

'I've missed you, little one,' she said.

'I've missed you too.'

That evening Jess went to write in her room, as she had countless times before. The late summer sun was shut out by her thick curtains. She sat down and selected a pen – purple ink this time.

'The Ice Boy', she wrote, but before she could go any further there came shouting from the street outside. She pulled the curtain aside – the sun was low, and lengthening shadows protected her from its light. A group of children were making their way down the centre of the road. The sandy-haired girl wasn't one of them, but she may as well have been, Jess thought. *They're all a bit the same, and I'm a bit different. I'm different, but that's good. That's me.*

Their chatter bubbled and popped, and for a second

she felt as hollow as she ever had. But when one of them looked up and caught her eye, she didn't shrink back. Instead she smiled. The girl smiled back, and went on her way.

His friend had gone and the ice boy was alone, she wrote, settling back to work. *Alone, just as he'd always been, but different too. He made a new bridge back to his home in the ice garden, which was easy because the world now bent and flexed at his touch. He closed up the crack in the wall and thought about what he might do.*

She tapped the base of her pen against the desk to get the ink, and her mind, flowing.

He had lived in the garden his whole life, too scared to go further. It was beautiful there. There were millions of flowers. There was fruit to eat. But now he'd had a taste of what lay beyond, he couldn't contain his curiosity. So he went back out into the world. He climbed to the top of the highest peak so he could look at the land from above. He followed the birds to their nesting places amongst the crags. Their eggs were spheres of ice, perfectly clear. He could see the fledglings inside, growing, changing, waiting to join their mothers.

He walked through the forest and slept amongst the vines. They drew him high into the canopy, where he could leap from branch to branch, far above the ground. There were animals there. There was life all around him and he learnt how to understand it. He saw so much. Ice-wolves running in packs across the tundra. Caves full of bats, millions of them, pouring out into the sky in a twisting silver column. Great beasts who carried their young in their mouths . . .

She went on, imagining the life her friend might now lead. He was out there, she knew. Just beyond her reach, but safe, and that thought made her glad.

When she looked up again, the colour was washing from the sky. There was a knock on the door downstairs.

'Jess, can you get that?' her mother called.

'I'm in my room!'

'Yes, I know that.'

'I'm not even Half Hat.'

'Then put it on!'

Jess sighed and trudged down, unfolding her sleeves and pulling the mask on. As she opened the door the setting sun made it impossible to see for a moment. But then she saw there was a boy standing on her doorstep.

'Davey!' she cried, and leapt forward, wrapping her arms around him before she even knew what she was doing.

'Thought I'd come and say hello. You've been so good visiting me all week, I reckoned it was my turn.' His voice was like a brass bell, booming out through the quiet of the street.

'They let you out!'

'They say I'll be fine as long as I don't get run over again.'

'Well, make sure you don't, then.'

'Try my best.'

'Do you want to come in? I was just writing a new story.'

'Actually, I thought you could come out.'

'Out? Me?'

'It's a nice evening and I've been lying around for ages, right?'

'I can't,' she said, and tapped her hood. 'I told you. I can't go out without this.'

'So just keep it on, then. No big deal, is it?'

'I don't know . . .'

'There's a playground down the other end of town. Got a massive slide in it. You can watch me go down head first and be impressed.'

'I can go head first too, thank you very much.'

'That's fine, as long as you're still impressed when I do it.'

The smile died on her lips. There was no way her mother would let her. She turned around, and there she was, leaning on the kitchen doorframe. Her face was tight and tense, but to Jess's surprise she nodded.

'Just for a little while, and then maybe Davey would like to stay for dinner?'

'I think my mum's cooking me tea, but I'll eat twice, no problem. Got to get my strength back, don't I? Just don't tell her.'

'Go on then, Jess. But be careful.'

The two of them stepped outside, one as thin as a rake in shorts and T-shirt, the other bundled up like a beekeeper. Clouds were like charcoal smudges in the darkening sky.

'I bet you I could win a race,' he said.

'I bet you couldn't.'

'We'll see about that.'

'All right, where's the finish line?'

'Right there at the end of the road. You've got no chance, though. I was hundred metres champion at my last school. Apart from the four guys who came ahead of me, that is.'

'Well, we'll see.'

'So it's a bet then?' Davey held out his hand to seal the bet, and when she took it there was a slight jolt of cold, like the echo of something past. For a moment she felt light-headed. There were connections there, just out of reach. And, she decided, that was all right.

'Go!' shouted Davey, and Jess sprinted after him.

The world rushed by, and she was part of it.

ACKNOWLEDGEMENTS

I owe a huge debt of gratitude to the many people who supported me in the writing of this book. My thanks firstly to Peter Buckman for his wise counsel in all matters. Secondly to the wonderful Kesia Lupo for her unflagging belief in the story and tireless efforts to make it better. To Barry Cunningham and Rachel Leyshon for their instincts, guidance, and for making this a reality. To Helen Crawford-White and Rachel Hickman for such a beautiful cover design. And of course to the rest of the team at Chicken House – Jazz, Elinor, Esther, Laura, Claire and Sarah.

Thanks too, go to Laura and Jamie Doward for the crucial role they played in this book seeing the light of day. To my parents and sister for their support and belief over the years. To the incredibly talented Ed Curtis, without whom I would never have become a writer. And lastly, a huge thank you to my wonderful wife, Sheba, for well . . . everything really.